PLANET NIGHTMARE

Start Publishing PD is a registered trademark of Start Publishing PD LLC
Manufactured in the United States of America

Cover art: Shutterstock/Taisiya Kozorez

Cover design: Jennifer Do

10 9 8 7 6 5 4 3 2 1

ISBN 979-8-8809-0993-3

PLANET NIGHTMARE

by Murray Leinster

TABLE OF CONTENTS

THE MAD PLANET

In All His lifetime of perhaps twenty years, it had never occurred to Burl to wonder what his grandfather had thought about his surroundings. The grandfather had come to an untimely end in a rather unpleasant fashion which Burl remembered vaguely as a succession of screams coming more and more faintly to his ears while he was being carried away at the top speed of which his mother was capable.

Burl had rarely or never thought of the old gentleman since. Surely he had never wondered in the abstract of what his great grandfather thought, and most surely of all, there never entered his head such a purely hypothetical question as the one of what his many-times-great-grandfather—say of the year 1920—would have thought of the scene in which Burl found himself.

He was treading cautiously over a brownish carpet of fungus growth, creeping furtively toward the stream which he knew by the generic title of "water." It was the only water he knew. Towering far above his head, three man-heights high, great toadstools hid the grayish sky from his sight. Clinging to the foot-thick stalks of the toadstools were still other fungi, parasites upon the growth that had once been parasites themselves.

Burl himself was a slender young man wearing a single garment twisted about his waist, made from the wing-fabric of a great moth the members of his tribe had slain as it emerged from its cocoon. His skin was fair, without a trace of sunburn. In all his lifetime he had never seen the sun, though the sky was rarely hidden from view save by the giant fungi which, with monster cabbages, were the only growing things he knew. Clouds usually spread overhead, and when they did not, the perpetual haze made the sun but an indefinitely brighter part of the sky, never a sharply edged ball of fire. Fantastic mosses, misshapen fungus growths, colossal molds and yeasts, were the essential parts of the landscape through which he moved.

Once as he had dodged through the forest of huge toadstools, his shoulder touched a cream-colored stalk, giving the whole fungus a tiny shock. Instantly, from the umbrella-like mass of pulp overhead, a fine and impalpable powder fell upon him like snow. It was the season when the toadstools sent out their spores, or seeds, and they had been dropped upon him at the first sign of disturbance.

6

Furtive as he was, he paused to brush them from his head and hair. They were deadly poison, as he knew well.

Burl would have been a curious sight to a man of the twentieth century. His skin was pink, like that of a child, and there was but little hair upon his body. Even that on top of his head was soft and downy. His chest was larger than his forefathers' had been, and his ears seemed almost capable of independent movement, to catch threatening sounds from any direction. His eyes, large and blue, possessed pupils which could dilate to extreme size, allowing him to see in almost complete darkness.

He was the result of the thirty thousand years' attempt of the human race to adapt itself to the change that had begun in the latter half of the twentieth century.

At about that time, civilization had been high, and apparently secure. Mankind had reached a permanent agreement among itself, and all men had equal opportunities to education and leisure. Machinery did most of the labor of the world, and men were only required to supervise its operation. All men were well-fed, all men were well-educated, and it seemed that until the end of time the earth would be the abode of a community of comfortable human beings, pursuing their studies and diversions, their illusions and their truths. Peace, quietness, privacy, freedom were universal.

Then, just when men were congratulating themselves that the Golden Age had come again, it was observed that the planet seemed ill at ease. Fissures opened slowly in the crust, and carbonic acid gas—the carbon dioxide of chemists—began to pour out into the atmosphere. That gas had long been known to be present in the air, and was considered necessary to plant life. Most of the plants of the world took the gas and absorbed its carbon into themselves, releasing the oxygen for use again.

Scientists had calculated that a great deal of the earth's increased fertility was due to the larger quantities of carbon dioxide released by the activities of man in burning his coal and petroleum. Because of those views, for some years no great alarm was caused by the continuous exhalation from the world's interior.

Constantly, however, the volume increased. New fissures constantly opened, each one adding a new source of carbon dioxide, and each one pouring into the already laden atmosphere more of the gas—beneficent in small quantities, but as the world learned, deadly in large ones.

The percentage of the heavy, vapor-like gas increased. The whole body of the air became heavier through its admixture. It absorbed more moisture and became more humid. Rainfall increased. Climates grew warmer. Vegetation became more luxuriant—but the air gradually became less exhilarating.

Soon the health of mankind began to be affected. Accustomed through long ages to breathe air rich in oxygen and poor in carbon dioxide, men suffered. Only those who lived on high plateaus or on tall mountaintops remained unaffected. The plants of the earth, though nourished and increasing in size beyond those ever seen before, were unable to dispose of the continually increasing flood of carbon dioxide.

*

By the middle of the twenty-first century it was generally recognized that a new carboniferous period was about to take place, when the earth's atmosphere would be thick and humid, unbreathable by man, when giant grasses and ferns would form the only vegetation.

When the twenty-first century drew to a close the whole human race began to revert to conditions closely approximating savagery. The lowlands were unbearable. Thick jungles of rank growth covered the ground. The air was depressing and enervating. Men could live there, but it was a sickly, fever-ridden existence. The whole population of the earth desired the high lands and as the low country became more unbearable, men forgot their two centuries of peace.

They fought destructively, each for a bit of land where he might live and breathe. Then men began to die, men who had persisted in remaining near sea-level. They could not live in the poisonous air. The danger zone crept up as the earth-fissures tirelessly poured out their steady streams of foul gas. Soon men could not live within five hundred feet of sea level. The lowlands went uncultivated, and became jungles of a thickness comparable only to those of the first carboniferous period.

Then men died of sheer inanition at a thousand feet. The plateaus and mountaintops were crowded with folk struggling for a foothold and food beyond the invisible menace that crept up, and up—

These things did not take place in one year, or in ten. Not in one generation, but in several. Between the time when the chemists of the International Geophysical Institute announced that the proportion of carbon dioxide in the air had increased from .04 per cent to .1 per cent and the time when at sea-level six per cent of the atmosphere was the deadly gas, more than two hundred years intervened.

Coming gradually, as it did, the poisonous effects of the deadly stuff increased with insidious slowness. First the lassitude, then the heaviness of brain, then the weakness of body. Mankind ceased to grow in numbers. After a long period, the race had fallen to a fraction of its former size. There was room in plenty on the mountaintops—but the danger-level continued to creep up.

There was but one solution. The human body would have to inure itself to the poison, or it was doomed to extinction. It finally developed a toleration for the gas that had wiped out race after race and nation after nation, but at a terrible cost. Lungs increased in size to secure the oxygen on which life depended, but the poison, inhaled at every breath, left the few survivors sickly and filled with a perpetual weariness. Their minds lacked the energy to cope with new problems or transmit the knowledge which in one degree or another, they possessed.

And after thirty thousand years, Burl, a direct descendant of the first president of the Universal Republic, crept through a forest of toadstools and fungus growths. He was ignorant of fire, or metals, of the uses of stone and wood. A single garment covered him. His language was a scanty group of a few hundred labial sounds, conveying no abstractions and few concrete things.

He was ignorant of the uses of wood. There was no wood in the scanty territory furtively inhabited by his tribe. With the increase in heat and humidity the trees had begun to die out. Those of northern climes went first, the oaks, the cedars, the maples. Then the pines—the beeches went early—the cypresses, and finally even the forests of the jungles vanished. Only grasses and reeds, bamboos and their kin, were able to flourish in the new, steaming atmosphere. The thick jungles gave place to dense thickets of grasses and ferns, now become treeferns again.

And then the fungi took their place. Flourishing as never before, flourishing on a planet of torrid heat and perpetual miasma, on whose surface the sun never shone directly because of an ever-thickening bank of clouds that hung sullenly overhead, the fungi sprang up. About the dank pools that festered over the surface of the earth, fungus growths began to cluster. Of every imaginable shade and color, of all monstrous forms and malignant purposes, of huge size and flabby volume, they spread over the land.

The grasses and ferns gave place to them. Squat footstools, flaking molds, evil-smelling yeasts, vast mounds of fungi inextricably mingled as to species, but growing, forever growing and exhaling an odor of dark places.

The strange growths now grouped themselves in forests, horrible travesties on the vegetation they had succeeded. They grew and grew with feverish intensity beneath a clouded or a haze-obscured sky, while above them fluttered gigantic butterflies and huge moths, sipping daintily of their corruption.

The insects alone of all the animal world above water, were able to endure the change. They multiplied exceedingly, and enlarged themselves in the thickened air. The solitary vegetation—as distinct from fungus growths—that had survived, was now a degenerate form of the cabbages that had once fed peasants. On those rank, colossal masses of foliage, the stolid grubs and caterpillars ate themselves to maturity, then swung below in strong cocoons to sleep the sleep of metamorphosis from which they emerged to spread their wings and fly.

The tiniest butterflies of former days had increased their span until their gaily colored wings should be described in terms of feet, while the larger emperor moths extended their purple sails to a breadth of yards upon yards. Burl himself would have been dwarfed beneath the overshadowing fabric of their wings.

It was fortunate that they, the largest flying creatures, were harmless or nearly so. Burl's fellow tribesmen sometimes came upon a cocoon just about to open, and waited patiently beside it until the beautiful creature within broke through its matted shell and came out into the sunlight.

Then, before it had gathered energy from the air, and before its wings had swelled to strength and firmness, the tribesmen fell upon it, tearing the filmy, delicate wings from its body and the limbs from its carcass. Then, when it lay helpless before them, they carried away the juicy, meat-filled limbs to be eaten, leaving the still living body to stare helplessly at this strange world through its many faceted eyes, and become a prey to the voracious ants who would soon clamber upon it and carry it away in tiny fragments to their underground city.

*

Not all the insect world was so helpless or so unthreatening. Burl knew of wasps almost the length of his own body who possessed stings that were instantly fatal. To every species of wasp, however, some other insect is predestined prey, and the furtive members of Burl's tribe feared them but little as they sought only the prey to which their instinct led them.

Bees were similarly aloof. They were hard put to it for existence, those bees. Few flowers bloomed, and they were reduced to expedients once considered signs of degeneracy in their race. Bubbling yeasts and fouler things, occasionally the nectarless blooms of the rank, giant cabbages. Burl knew the bees. They droned overhead, nearly as large as he was himself, their bulging eyes gazing at him with abstracted preoccupation. And crickets, and beetles, and spiders—

Burl knew spiders! His grandfather had been the prey of one of the hunting tarantulas, which had leaped with incredible ferocity from his excavated tunnel in the earth. A vertical pit in the ground, two feet in diameter, went down for twenty feet. At the bottom of that lair the black-bellied monster waited for the tiny sounds that would warn him of prey approaching his hiding-place (*Lycosa fasciata*).

Burl's grandfather had been careless, and the terrible shrieks he uttered as the horrible monster darted from the pit and seized him had lingered vaguely in Burl's mind ever since. Burl had seen, too, the monster webs of another species of spider, and watched from a safe distance as the misshapen body of the huge creature sucked the juices from a three-foot cricket that had become entangled in its trap.

Burl had remembered the strange stripes of yellow and black and silver that crossed upon its abdomen (*Epiera fasciata*). He had been fascinated by the struggles of the imprisoned insect, coiled in a hopeless tangle of sticky, gummy ropes the thickness of Burl's finger, cast about its body before the spider made any attempt to approach.

Burl knew these dangers. They were a part of his life. It was his accustomedness to them, and that of his ancestors, that made his existence possible. He was able to evade them; so he survived. A moment of carelessness, an instant's relaxation of his habitual caution, and he would be one with his forebears, forgotten meals of long-dead, inhuman monsters.

Three days before, Burl had crouched behind a bulky, shapeless fungus growth while he watched a furious duel between two huge horned beetles. Their jaws, gaping wide, clicked and clashed upon each other's impenetrable armor. Their legs crashed like so many cymbals as their polished surfaces ground and struck against each other. They were fighting over some particularly attractive bit of carrion.

Burl had watched with all his eyes until a gaping orifice appeared in the armor of the smaller of the two. It uttered a shrill cry, or seemed to cry out. The noise was, actually, the tearing of the horny stuff beneath the victorious jaws of the adversary.

The wounded beetle struggled more and more feebly. At last it collapsed, and the conqueror placidly began to eat the conquered before life was extinct.

Burl waited until the meal was finished, and then approached the scene with caution. An ant—the forerunner of many—was already inspecting the carcass.

Burl usually ignored the ants. They were stupid, short-sighted insects, and not hunters. Save when attacked, they offered no injury. They were scavengers, on the lookout for the dead and dying, but they would fight viciously if their prey were questioned, and they were dangerous opponents. They were from three inches, for the tiny black ants, to a foot for the large termites.

Burl was hasty when he heard the tiny clickings of their limbs as they approached. He seized the sharp-pointed snout of the victim, detached from the body, and fled from the scene.

Later, he inspected his find with curiosity. The smaller victim had been a minotaur beetle, with a sharp-pointed horn like that of a rhinoceros to reinforce his offensive armament, already dangerous because of his wide jaws. The jaws of a beetle work from side to side, instead of up and down, and this had made the protection complete in no less than three directions.

Burl inspected the sharp, dagger-like instrument in his hand. He felt its point, and it pricked his finger. He flung it aside as he crept to the hiding-place of his tribe. There were only twenty of them, four or five men, six or seven women, and the rest girls and children.

Burl had been wondering at the strange feelings that came over him when he looked at one of the girls. She was younger than Burl—perhaps eighteen—and fleeter of foot than he. They talked together, sometimes, and once or twice Burl shared with her an especially succulent find of foodstuffs.

*

The next morning he found the horn where he had thrown it, sticking in the flabby side of a toadstool. He pulled it out, and gradually, far back in his mind, an idea began to take shape. He sat for some time with the thing in his hand, considering it with a far-away look in his eyes. From time to time he stabbed at a toadstool, awkwardly, but with gathering skill. His imagination began to work fitfully. He visualized himself stabbing food with it as the larger beetle had stabbed the former owner of the weapon he had in his hand.

Burl could not imagine himself coping with one of the fighting insects. He could only picture himself, dimly, stabbing something that was food with this death-dealing thing. It was no longer than his arm and though clumsy to the hand, an effective and terribly sharp implement.

He thought: Where was there food, food that lived, that would not fight back? Presently he rose and began to make his way toward the tiny river. Yellow-bellied newts swam in its waters. The swimming larvae of a thousand insects floated about its surface or crawled upon its bottom.

There were deadly things there, too. Giant crayfish snapped their horny claws at the unwary. Mosquitoes of four-inch wing-spread sometimes made their humming way above the river. The last survivors of their race, they were dying out for lack of the plant-juices on which the male of the species lived, but even so they were formidable. Burl had learned to crush them with fragments of fungus.

He crept slowly through the forest of toadstools. Brownish fungus was underfoot. Strange orange, red, and purple molds clustered about the bases of the creamy toadstool stalks. Once Burl paused to run his sharp-pointed weapon through a fleshy stalk and reassure himself that what he planned was practicable.

He made his way furtively through the forest of misshapen growths. Once he heard a tiny clicking, and froze into stillness. It was a troop of four or five ants, each some eight inches long, returning along their habitual pathway to their city. They moved sturdily, heavily laden, along the route marked with the black and odorous formic acid exuded from the bodies of their comrades. Burl waited until they had passed, then went on.

He came to the bank of the river. Green scum covered a great deal of its surface, scum occasionally broken by a slowly enlarging bubble of some gas released from decomposing matter on the bottom. In the center of the placid stream the current ran a little more swiftly, and the water itself was visible.

Over the shining current, water-spiders ran swiftly. They had not shared in the general increase of size that had taken place in the insect world. Depending upon the capillary qualities of the water to support them, an increase in size and weight would have deprived them of the means of locomotion.

From the spot where Burl first peered at the water the green scum spread out for many yards into the stream. He could not see what swam and wriggled and crawled beneath the evil-smelling covering. He peered up and down the banks.

Perhaps a hundred and fifty yards below, the current came near the shore. An outcropping of rock there made a steep descent to the river, from which yellow shelf-fungi stretched out. Dark red and orange above, they were light yellow below, and they formed a series of platforms above the smoothly flowing stream. Burl made his way cautiously toward them.

On his way he saw one of the edible mushrooms that formed so large a part of his diet, and paused to break from the flabby flesh an amount that would feed him for many days. It was too often the custom of his people to find a store of food, carry it to their hiding place, and then gorge themselves for days, eating, sleeping, and waking only to eat again until the food was gone.

Absorbed as he was in his plan of trying his new weapon, Burl was tempted to return with his booty. He would give Saya of this food, and they would eat together. Saya was the maiden who roused unusual emotions in Burl. He felt strange impulses stirring within him when she was near, a desire to touch her, to caress her. He did not understand.

He went on, after hesitating. If he brought her food, Saya would be pleased, but if he brought her of the things that swam in the stream, she would be still more pleased. Degraded as his tribe had become, Burl was yet a little more intelligent than they. He was an atavism, a throwback to ancestors who had cultivated the earth and subjugated its animals. He had a vague idea of pride, unformed but potent.

No man within memory had hunted or slain for food. They knew of meat, yes, but it had been the fragments left by an insect hunter, seized and carried away by the men before the perpetually alert ant colonies had sent their foragers to the scene.

If Burl did what no man before him had done, if he brought a whole carcass to his tribe, they would envy him. They were preoccupied solely with their stomachs, and after that with the preservation of their lives. The perpetuation of the race came third in their consideration.

They were herded together in a leaderless group, coming to the same hiding place that they might share in the finds of the lucky and gather comfort from their numbers. Of weapons, they had none. They sometimes used stones to crack open the limbs of the huge insects they found partly devoured, cracking them open for the sweet meat to be found inside, but they sought safety from their enemies solely in flight and hiding.

Their enemies were not as numerous as might have been imagined. Most of the meat-eating insects have their allotted prey. The sphex—a hunting wasp—feeds solely upon grasshoppers. Others wasps eat flies only. The pirate-bee eats bumblebees only. Spiders were the principal enemies of man, as they devour with a terrifying impartiality all that falls into their clutches.

Burl reached the spot from which he might gaze down into the water. He lay prostrate, staring into the shallow depths. Once a huge crayfish, as long as Burl's body, moved leisurely across his vision. Small fishes and even the huge newts fled before the voracious creature.

After a long time the tide of underwater life resumed its activity. The wriggling grubs of the dragonflies reappeared. Little flecks of silver swam into view—a school of tiny fish. A larger fish appeared, moving slowly through the water.

Burl's eyes glistened and his mouth watered. He reached down with his long weapon. It barely touched the water. Disappointment filled him, yet the nearness and the apparent practicability of his scheme spurred him on.

He considered the situation. There were the shelf-fungi below him. He rose and moved to a point just above them, then thrust his spear down.

PLANET NIGHTMARE

They resisted its point. Burl felt them tentatively with his foot, then dared to thrust his weight to them. They held him firmly. He clambered down and lay flat upon them, peering over the edge as before.

The large fish, as long as Burl's arm, swam slowly to and fro below him. Burl had seen the former owner of his spear strive to thrust it into his opponents, and knew that a thrust was necessary. He had tried his weapon upon toadstools—had practiced with it. When the fish swam below him, he thrust sharply downward. The spear seemed to bend when it entered the water, and missed its mark by inches, to Burl's astonishment. He tried again and again.

He grew angry with the fish below him for eluding his efforts to kill it. Repeated strokes had left it untouched, and it was unwary, and did not even try to run away.

Burl became furious. The big fish came to rest directly beneath his hand. Burl thrust downward with all his strength. This time the spear, entering vertically, did not seem to bend. It went straight down. Its point penetrated the scales of the swimmer below, transfixing that lazy fish completely.

An uproar began. The fish, struggling to escape, and Burl, trying to draw it up to his perch, made a huge commotion. In his excitement Burl did not observe a tiny ripple some distance away. The monster crayfish was attracted by the disturbance, and was approaching.

The unequal combat continued. Burl hung on desperately to the end of his spear. Then there was a tremor in Burl's support, it gave way, and fell into the stream with a mighty splash. Burl went under, his eyes open, facing death. And as he sank, his wide-open eyes saw waved before him the gaping claws of the huge crayfish, large enough to sever a limb with a single stroke of their jagged jaws.

*

He opened his mouth to scream—a replica of the terrible screams of his grandfather, seized by a black-bellied tarantula years before—but no sound came forth. Only bubbles floated to the surface of the water. He beat the unresisting fluid with his hands—he did not know how to swim. The colossal creature approached leisurely, while Burl struggled helplessly.

His arms struck a solid object, and grasped it convulsively. A second later he had swung it between himself and the huge crustacean. He felt a

16

shock as the mighty jaws closed upon the corklike fungus, then felt himself drawn upward as the crayfish released his hold and the shelf-fungus floated to the surface. Having given way beneath him, it had been carried below him in his fall, only to rise within his reach just when most needed.

Burl's head popped above water and he saw a larger bit of the fungus floating near by. Less securely anchored to the rocks of the river bank than the shelf to which Burl had trusted himself, it had been dislodged when the first shelf gave way. It was larger than the fragment to which Burl clung, and floated higher in the water.

Burl was cool with a terrible self-possession. He seized it and struggled to draw himself on top of it. It tilted as his weight came upon it, and nearly overturned, but he paid no heed. With desperate haste, he clawed with hands and feet until he could draw himself clear of the water, of which he would forever retain a slight fear.

As he pulled himself upon the furry, orange-brown upper surface, a sharp blow struck his foot. The crayfish, disgusted at finding only what was to it a tasteless morsel in the shelf-fungus, had made a languid stroke at Burl's wriggling foot in the water. Failing to grasp the fleshy member, the crayfish retreated, disgruntled and annoyed.

And Burl floated downstream, perched, weaponless and alone, frightened and in constant danger, upon a flimsy raft composed of a degenerate fungus floating soggily in the water. He floated slowly down the stream of a river in whose waters death lurked unseen, upon whose banks was peril, and above whose reaches danger fluttered on golden wings.

It was a long time before he recovered his self-possession, and when he did he looked first for his spear. It was floating in the water, still transfixing the fish whose capture had endangered Burl's life. The fish now floated with its belly upward, all life gone.

So insistent was Burl's instinct for food that his predicament was forgotten when he saw his prey just out of his reach. He gazed at it, and his mouth watered, while his cranky craft went downstream, spinning slowly in the current. He lay flat on the floating fungoid, and strove to reach out and grasp the end of the spear.

The raft tilted and nearly flung him overboard again. A little later he discovered that it sank more readily on one side than on the other. That was due, of course, to the greater thickness—and consequently greater buoyancy—of the part which had grown next the rocks of the river bank.

Burl found that if he lay with his head stretching above that side, it did not sink into the water. He wriggled into this new position, then, and waited until the slow revolution of his vessel brought the spear-shaft near him. He stretched his fingers and his arm, and touched, then grasped it.

A moment later he was tearing strips of flesh from the side of the fish and cramming the oily mess into his mouth with great enjoyment. He had lost his edible mushroom. That danced upon the waves several yards away, but Burl ate contentedly of what he possessed. He did not worry about what was before him. That lay in the future, but suddenly he realized that he was being carried farther and farther from Saya, the maiden of his tribe who caused strange bliss to steal over him when he contemplated her.

The thought came to him when he visualized the delight with which she would receive a gift of part of the fish he had caught. He was suddenly stricken with dumb sorrow. He lifted his head and looked longingly at the river banks.

A long, monotonous row of strangely colored fungus growths. No healthy green, but pallid, cream-colored toadstools, some bright orange, lavender, and purple molds, vivid carmine "rusts" and mildews, spreading up the banks from the turgid slime. The sun was not a ball of fire, but merely shone as a bright golden patch in the haze-filled sky, a patch whose limits could not be defined or marked.

In the faintly pinkish light that filtered down through the air, a multitude of flying objects could be seen. Now and then a cricket or a grasshopper made its bullet-like flight from one spot to another. Huge butterflies fluttered gayly above the silent, seemingly lifeless world. Bees lumbered anxiously about, seeking the cross-shaped flowers of the monster cabbages. Now and then a slender-waisted, yellow-stomached wasp flew alertly through the air.

Burl watched them with a strange indifference. The wasps were as long as he himself. The bees, on end, could match his height. The butterflies ranged from tiny creatures barely capable of shading his face to colossal things in the folds of whose wings he could have been lost. And above him fluttered dragonflies, whose long, spindle-like bodies were three times the length of his own.

Burl ignored them all. Sitting there, an incongruous creature of pink skin and soft brown hair upon an orange fungus floating in midstream, he was filled with despondency because the current carried him forever farther and farther from a certain slender-limbed maiden of his tiny tribe, whose glances caused an odd commotion in his breast.

*

The day went on. Once, Burl saw upon the blue-green mold that spread upward from the river, a band of large, red Amazon ants, marching in orderly array, to raid the city of a colony of black ants, and carry away the eggs they would find there. The eggs would be hatched, and the small black creatures made the slaves of the brigands who had stolen them.

The Amazon ants can live only by the labor of their slaves, and for that reason are mighty warriors in their world. Later, etched against the steaming mist that overhung everything as far as the eye could reach, Burl saw strangely shaped, swollen branches rearing themselves from the ground. He knew what they were. A hard-rinded fungus that grew upon itself in peculiar mockery of the vegetation that had vanished from the earth.

And again he saw pear-shaped objects above some of which floated little clouds of smoke. They, too, were fungus growths, puffballs, which when touched emit what seems a puff of vapor. These would have towered above Burl's head, had he stood beside them.

And then, as the day drew to an end, he saw in the distance what seemed a range of purple hills. They were tall hills to Burl, some sixty or seventy feet high, and they seemed to be the agglomeration of a formless growth, multiplying its organisms and forms upon itself until the whole formed an irregular, cone-shaped mound. Burl watched them apathetically.

Presently, he ate again of the oily fish. The taste was pleasant to him, accustomed to feed mostly upon insipid mushrooms. He stuffed himself, though the size of his prey left by far the larger part uneaten.

He still held his spear firmly beside him.

It had brought him into trouble, but Burl possessed a fund of obstinacy. Unlike most of his tribe, he associated the spear with the food it had secured, rather than the difficulty into which it had led him. When he had eaten his fill he picked it up and examined it again. The sharpness of its point was unimpaired.

Burl handled it meditatively, debating whether or not to attempt to fish again. The shakiness of his little raft dissuaded him, and he abandoned the idea. Presently he stripped a sinew from the garment about his middle and hung the fish about his neck with it. That would leave him both hands free. Then he sat cross-legged upon the soggily floating fungus, like a pink-skinned Buddha, and watched the shores go by.

Time had passed, and it was drawing near sunset. Burl, never having seen the sun save as a bright spot in the overhanging haze, did not think of the coming of night as "sunset." To him it was the letting down of darkness from the sky.

Today happened to be an exceptionally bright day, and the haze was not as thick as usual. Far to the west, the thick mist turned to gold, while the thicker clouds above became blurred masses of dull red. Their shadows seemed like lavender, from the contrast of shades. Upon the still surface of the river, all the myriad tints and shadings were reflected with an incredible faithfulness, and the shining tops of the giant mushrooms by the river brim glowed faintly pink.

Dragonflies buzzed over his head in their swift and angular flight, the metallic luster of their bodies glistening in the rosy light. Great yellow butterflies flew lightly above the stream. Here, there, and everywhere upon the water appeared the shell-formed boats of a thousand caddis flies, floating upon the surface while they might.

Burl could have thrust his hand down into their cavities and seized the white worms that inhabited the strange craft. The huge bulk of a tardy bee droned heavily overhead. Burl glanced upward and saw the long proboscis and the hairy hinder legs with their scanty load of pollen. He saw the great, multiple-lensed eyes with their expression of stupid preoccupation, and even the sting that would mean death alike for him and for the giant insect, should it be used.

The crimson radiance grew dim at the edge of the world. The purple hills had long been left behind. Now the slender stalks of ten thousand round-domed mushrooms lined the river bank and beneath them spread fungi of all colors, from the rawest red to palest blue, but all now fading slowly to a monochromatic background in the growing dusk.

The buzzing, fluttering, and the flapping of the insects of the day died slowly down, while from a million hiding places there crept out into the deep night soft and furry bodies of great moths, who preened themselves and smoothed their feathery antennae before taking to the air. The strong-limbed crickets set up their thunderous noise—grown gravely bass with the increasing size of the organs by which the sound was made—and then there began to gather on the water those slender spirals of tenuous mist that would presently blanket the stream in a mantle of thin fog.

*

Night fell. The clouds above seemed to lower and grow dark. Gradually, now a drop and then a drop, now a drop and then a drop, the languid fall of large, warm raindrops that would drip from the moisture-laden skies all through the night began. The edge of the stream became a place where great disks of coolly glowing flame appeared.

The mushrooms that bordered on the river were faintly phosphorescent (*Pleurotus phosphoreus*) and shone coldly upon the "rusts" and flake-fungi beneath their feet. Here and there a ball of lambent flame appeared, drifting idly above the steaming, festering earth.

Thirty thousand years before, men had called them "will-o'-the-wisps," but Burl simply stared at them, accepting them as he accepted all that passed. Only a man attempting to advance in the scale of civilization tries to explain everything that he sees. The savage and the child is most often content to observe without comment, unless he repeats the legends told him by wise folk who are possessed by the itch of knowledge.

Burl watched for a long time. Great fireflies whose beacons lighted up their surroundings for many yards—fireflies Burl knew to be as long as his spear—shed their intermittent glows upon the stream. Softly fluttering wings, in great beats that poured torrents of air upon him, passed above Burl.

The air was full of winged creatures. The night was broken by their cries, by the sound of their invisible wings, by their cries of anguish and their mating calls. Above him and on all sides the persistent, intense life of the insect world went on ceaselessly, but Burl rocked back and forth upon his frail mushroom boat and wished to weep because he was being carried from his tribe, and from Saya—Saya of the swift feet and white teeth, of the shy smile.

Burl may have been homesick, but his principal thoughts were of Saya. He had dared greatly to bring a gift of fresh meat to her, meat captured as meat had never been known to be taken by a member of the tribe. And now he was being carried from her!

He lay, disconsolate, upon his floating atom on the water for a great part of the night. It was long after midnight when the mushroom raft struck gently and remained grounded upon a shallow in the stream.

When the light came in the morning, Burl gazed about him keenly. He was some twenty yards from the shore, and the greenish scum surrounded his now disintegrating vessel. The river had widened out until the other bank was barely to be seen through the haze above the surface of the river, but the nearer shore seemed firm and no more full of dangers than the territory his tribe inhabited. He felt the depth of the water with his spear, then was struck with the multiple usefulness of that weapon. The water would come to but slightly above his ankles.

Shivering a little with fear, Burl stepped down into the water, then made for the bank at the top of his speed. He felt a soft something clinging to one of his bare feet. With an access of terror, he ran faster, and stumbled upon the shore in a panic. He stared down at his foot. A shapeless, flesh-colored pad clung to his heel, and as Burl watched, it began to swell slowly, while the pink of its wrinkled folds deepened.

It was no more than a leech, sharing in the enlargement nearly all the lower world had undergone, but Burl did not know that. He thrust at it with the side of his spear, then scraped frantically at it, and it fell off, leaving a blotch of blood upon the skin where it came away. It lay, writhing and pulsating, upon the ground, and Burl fled from it.

He found himself in one of the toadstool forests with which he was familiar, and finally paused, disconsolately. He knew the nature of the fungus growths about him, and presently fell to eating. In Burl the sight of food always produced hunger—a wise provision of nature to make up for the instinct to store food, which he lacked.

Burl's heart was small within him. He was far from his tribe, and far from Saya. In the parlance of this day, it is probable that no more than forty miles separated them, but Burl did not think of distances. He had come down the river. He was in a land he had never known or seen. And he was alone.

All about him was food. All the mushrooms that surrounded him were edible, and formed a store of sustenance Burl's whole tribe could not have eaten in many days, but that very fact brought Saya to his mind more forcibly. He squatted on the ground, wolfing down the insipid mushroom in great gulps, when an idea suddenly came to him with all the force of inspiration.

He would bring Saya here, where there was food, food in great quantities, and she would be pleased. Burl had forgotten the large and oily fish that still hung down his back from the sinew about his neck, but now he rose, and its flapping against him reminded him again.

He took it and fingered it all over, getting his hands and himself thoroughly greasy in the process, but he could eat no more. The thought of Saya's pleasure at the sight of that, too, reinforced his determination.

With all the immediacy of a child or a savage he set off at once. He had come along the bank of the stream. He would retrace his steps along the bank of the stream.

Through the awkward aisles of the mushroom forest he made his way, eyes and ears open for possibilities of danger. Several times he heard the omnipresent clicking of ants on their multifarious businesses in the wood, but he could afford to ignore them. They were short-sighted at best, and at worst they were foragers rather than hunters. He only feared one kind of ant, the army-ant, which sometimes travels in hordes of millions, eating all that it comes upon. In ages past, when they were tiny creatures not an inch long, even the largest animals fled from them. Now that they measured a foot in length, not even the gorged spiders whose distended bellies were a yard in thickness, dared offer them battle.

The mushroom forest came to an end. A cheerful grasshopper (*Ephigger*) munched delicately at some dainty it had found. Its hind legs were bunched beneath it in perpetual readiness for flight. A monster wasp appeared above—as long as Burl himself—poised an instant, dropped, and seized the luckless feaster.

There was a struggle, then the grasshopper became helpless, and the wasp's flexible abdomen curved delicately. Its sting entered the jointed armor of its prey, just beneath the head. The sting entered with all the deliberate precision of a surgeon's scalpel, and all struggle ceased.

The wasp grasped the paralyzed, not dead, insect and flew away. Burl grunted, and passed on. He had hidden when the wasp darted down from above.

23

PLANET NIGHTMARE

The ground grew rough, and Burl's progress became painful. He clambered arduously up steep slopes and made his way cautiously down their farther sides. Once he had to climb through a tangled mass of mushrooms so closely placed, and so small, that he had to break them apart with blows of his spear before he could pass, when they shed upon him torrents of a fiery red liquid that rolled off his greasy breast and sank into the ground (*Lactarius deliciosus*).

A strange self-confidence now took possession of Burl. He walked less cautiously and more boldly. The mere fact that he had struck something and destroyed it provided him with a curious fictitious courage.

He had climbed slowly to the top of a red clay cliff, perhaps a hundred feet high, slowly eaten away by the river when it overflowed. Burl could see the river. At some past floodtime it had lapped at the base of the cliff on whose edge he walked, though now it came no nearer than a quarter-mile.

The cliffside was almost covered with shelf-fungi, large and small, white, yellow, orange, and green, in indescribable confusion and luxuriance. From a point halfway up the cliff the inch-thick cable of a spider's web stretched down to an anchorage on the ground, and the strangely geometrical pattern of the web glistened evilly.

Somewhere among the fungi of the cliffside the huge creature waited until some unfortunate prey should struggle helplessly in its monster snare. The spider waited in a motionless, implacable patience, invincibly certain of prey, utterly merciless to its victims.

Burl strutted on the edge of the cliff, a silly little pink-skinned creature with an oily fish slung about his neck and a draggled fragment of a moth's wing about his middle. In his hand he bore the long spear of a minotaur beetle. He strutted, and looked scornfully down upon the whitely shining trap below him. He struck mushrooms, and they had fallen before him. He feared nothing. He strode fearlessly along. He would go to Saya and bring her to this land where food grew in abundance.

Sixty paces before him, a shaft sank vertically in the sandy, clayey soil. It was a carefully rounded shaft, and lined with silk. It went down for perhaps thirty feet or more, and there enlarged itself into a chamber where the owner and digger of the shaft might rest. The top of the hole was closed by a trap door, stained with mud and earth to imitate with precision the surrounding soil. A keen eye would have been needed to perceive the opening. But a keen eye now peered out from a tiny crack, the eye of the engineer of the underground dwelling.

Eight hairy legs surrounded the body of the creature that hung motionless at the top of the silk-lined shaft. A huge misshapen globe formed its body, colored a dirty brown. Two pairs of ferocious mandibles stretched before its fierce mouth-parts. Two eyes glittered evilly in the darkness of the burrow. And over the whole body spread a rough, mangy fur.

It was a thing of implacable malignance, of incredible ferocity. It was the brown hunting-spider, the American tarantula (*Mygale Hentzii*). Its body was two feet and more in diameter, and its legs, outstretched, would cover a circle three yards across. It watched Burl, its eyes glistening. Slaver welled up and dropped from its jaws.

And Burl strutted forward on the edge of the cliff, puffed up with a sense of his own importance. The white snare of the spinning spider below him impressed him as amusing. He knew the spider would not leave its web to attack him. He reached down and broke off a bit of fungus growing at his feet. Where he broke it, it was oozing a soupy liquid and was full of tiny maggots in a delirium of feasting. Burl flung it down into the web, and then laughed as the black bulk of the hidden spider swung down from its hiding place to investigate.

*

The tarantula, peering from its burrow, quivered with impatience. Burl drew near, and nearer. He was using his spear as a lever, now, and prying off bits of fungus to fall down the cliffside into the colossal web. The spider, below, went leisurely from one place to another, investigating each new missile with its palpi, then leaving them, as they appeared lifeless and undesirable prey. Burl laughed again as a particularly large lump of shelf-fungus narrowly missed the black-and-silver figure below. Then—

The trap door fell into place with a faint click, and Burl whirled about. His laughter turned to a scream. Moving toward him with incredible rapidity, the monster tarantula opened its dripping jaws. Its mandibles gaped wide. The poison fangs were unsheathed. The creature was thirty paces away, twenty paces—ten. It leaped into the air, eyes glittering, all its eight legs extended to seize, fangs bared—

Burl screamed again, and thrust out his arms to ward off the impact of the leap. In his terror, his grasp upon his spear had become agonized. The spear point shot out, and the tarantula fell upon it. Nearly a quarter of the spear entered the body of the ferocious thing.

It struck upon the spear, writhing horribly, still struggling to reach Burl, who was transfixed with horror. The mandibles clashed, strange sounds came from the beast. Then one of the attenuated, hairy legs rasped across Burl's forearm. He gasped in ultimate fear and stepped backward—and the edge of the cliff gave way beneath him.

He hurtled downward, still clutching the spear which led the writhing creature from him. Down through space, eyes glassy with panic, the two creatures—the man and the giant tarantula—fell together. There was a strangely elastic crash and crackling. They had fallen into the web beneath them.

Burl had reached the end of terror. He could be no more fear-struck. Struggling madly in the gummy coils of an immense web, which ever bound him more tightly, with a wounded creature shuddering in agony not a yard from him—yet a wounded creature that still strove to reach him with its poison fangs—Burl had reached the limit of panic.

He fought like a madman to break the coils about him. His arms and breast were greasy from the oily fish, and the sticky web did not adhere to them, but his legs and body were inextricably fastened by the elastic threads spread for just such prey as he.

He paused a moment, in exhaustion. Then he saw, five yards away, the silvery and black monster waiting patiently for him to weary himself. It judged the moment propitious. The tarantula and the man were one in its eyes, one struggling thing that had fallen opportunely into its snare. They were moving but feebly now. The spider advanced delicately, swinging its huge bulk nimbly along the web, paying out a cable after it came inexorably toward him.

Burl's arms were free, because of the greasy coating they had received. He waved them wildly, shrieking at the pitiless monster that approached. The spider paused. Those moving arms suggested mandibles that might wound or slap.

Spiders take few hazards. This spider was no exception to the rule. It drew cautiously near, then stopped. Its spinnerets became busy, and with one of its six legs, used like an arm, it flung a sheet of gummy silk impartially over both the tarantula and the man.

26

Burl fought against the descending shroud. He strove to thrust it away, but in vain. In a matter of minutes he was completely covered in a silken cloth that hid even the light from his eyes. He and his enemy, the giant tarantula, were beneath the same covering, though the tarantula moved but weakly.

The shower ceased. The web-spider had decided that they were helpless. Then Burl felt the cables of the web give slightly, as the spider approached to sting and suck the sweet juices from its prey.

*

The web yielded gently as the added weight of the black-bellied spider approached. Burl froze into stillness under his enveloping covering. Beneath the same silken shroud the tarantula writhed in agony upon the point of Burl's spear. It clashed its jaws, shuddering upon the horny barb.

Burl was quiet in an ecstasy of terror. He waited for the poison-fangs to be thrust into him. He knew the process. He had seen the leisurely fashion in which the giant spiders delicately stung their prey, then withdrew to wait without impatience for the poison to do its work.

When their victim had ceased to struggle, they drew near again, and sucked the sweet juices from the body, first from one point and then another, until what had so recently been a creature vibrant with life became a shrunken, withered husk—to be flung from the web at nightfall. Most spiders are tidy housekeepers, destroying their snares daily to spin anew.

The bloated, evil creature moved meditatively about the shining sheet of silk it had cast over the man and the giant tarantula when they fell from the cliff above. Now only the tarantula moved feebly. Its body was outlined by a bulge in the concealing shroud, throbbing faintly as it still struggled with the spear in its vitals. The irregularly rounded protuberance offered a point of attack for the web spider. It moved quickly forward, and stung.

Galvanized into fresh torment by this new agony, the tarantula writhed in a very hell of pain. Its legs, clustered about the spear still fastened into its body, struck out purposelessly, in horrible gestures of delirious suffering. Burl screamed as one of them touched him, and struggled himself.

His arms and head were free beneath the silken sheet because of the grease and oil that coated them. He clutched at the threads about him and strove to draw himself away from his deadly neighbor. The threads did not break, but they parted one from another, and a tiny opening appeared. One of the tarantula's attenuated limbs touched him again. With the strength of utter panic he hauled himself away, and the opening enlarged. Another struggle, and Burl's head emerged into the open air, and he stared down for twenty feet upon an open space almost carpeted with the chitinous remains of his present captor's former victims.

Burl's head was free, and his breast and arms. The fish slung over his shoulder had shed its oil upon him impartially. But the lower part of his body was held firm by the gummy snare of the web-spider, a snare far more tenacious than any bird-lime ever manufactured by man.

He hung in his tiny window for a moment, despairing. Then he saw, at a little distance, the bulk of the monster spider, waiting patiently for its poison to take effect and the struggling of its prey to be stilled. The tarantula was no more than shuddering now. Soon it would be still, and the black-bellied creature waiting on the web would approach for its meal.

Burl withdrew his head and thrust desperately at the sticky stuff about his loins and legs. The oil upon his hands kept it from clinging to them, and it gave a little. In a flash of inspiration, Burl understood. He reached over his shoulder and grasped the greasy fish; tore it in a dozen places and smeared himself with the now rancid exudation, pushing the sticky threads from his limbs and oiling the surface from which he had thrust it away.

He felt the web tremble. To the spider, its poison seemed to have failed of effect. Another sting seemed to be necessary. This time it would not insert its fangs into the quiescent tarantula, but would sting where the disturbance was manifest—would send its deadly venom into Burl.

He gasped, and drew himself toward his window. It was as if he would have pulled his legs from his body. His head emerged, his shoulders—half his body was out of the hole.

The colossal spider surveyed him, and made ready to cast more of its silken sheet upon him. The spinnerets became active, and the sticky stuff about Burl's feet gave way! He shot out of the opening and fell sprawling, awkwardly and heavily, upon the earth below, crashing upon the shrunken shell of a flying beetle which had fallen into the snare and had not escaped.

MURRAY LEINSTER

Burl rolled over and over, and then sat up. An angry, foot-long ant stood before him, its mandibles extended threateningly, while its antennae waved wildly in the air. A shrill stridulation filled the air.

In ages past, when ants were tiny creatures of lengths to be measured in fractions of an inch, learned scientists debated gravely if their tribe possessed a cry. They believed that certain grooves upon the body of the insects, after the fashion of those upon the great legs of the cricket, might offer the means of uttering an infinitely high-pitched sound too shrill for man's ears to catch.

Burl knew that the stridulation was caused by the doubtful insect before him, though he had never wondered how it was produced. The cry was used to summon others of its city, to help it in its difficulty or good fortune.

Clickings sounded fifty or sixty feet away. Comrades were coming to aid the pioneer. Harmless save when interfered with—all save the army ant, that is—the whole ant tribe was formidable when aroused. Utterly fearless, they could pull down a man and slay him as so many infuriated fox terriers might have done thirty thousand years before.

*

Burl fled, without debate, and nearly collided with one of the anchoring cables of the web from which he had barely escaped a moment before. He heard the shrill sound behind him suddenly subside. The ant, short-sighted as all ants were, no longer felt itself threatened and went peacefully about the business Burl had interrupted, that of finding among the gruesome relics beneath the spider's web some edible carrion which might feed the inhabitants of its city.

Burl sped on for a few hundred yards, and stopped. It behooved him to move carefully. He was in strange territory, and as even the most familiar territory was full of sudden and implacable dangers, unknown lands were doubly or trebly perilous.

Burl, too found difficulty in moving. The glutinous stuff from the spider's shroud of silk still stuck to his feet and picked up small objects as he went along. Old ant-gnawed fragments of insect armour pricked him even through his toughened soles.

He looked about cautiously and removed them, took a dozen steps and had to stop again. Burl's brain had been uncommonly stimulated of late.

PLANET NIGHTMARE

It had gotten him into at least one predicament—due to his invention of a spear—but had no less readily led to his escape from another. But for the reasoning that had led him to use the grease from the fish upon his shoulder in oiling his body when he struggled out of the spider's snare, he would now be furnishing a meal for that monster.

Cautiously, Burl looked all about him. He seemed to be safe. Then, quite deliberately, he sat down to think. It was the first time in his life that he had done such a thing. The people of his tribe were not given to meditation. But an idea had struck Burl with all the force of inspiration—an abstract idea.

When he was in difficulties, something within him seemed to suggest a way out. Would it suggest an inspiration now? He puzzled over the problem. Childlike—and savage-like—the instant the thought came to him, he proceeded to test it out. He fixed his gaze upon his foot. The sharp edges of pebbles, of the remains of insect-armour, of a dozen things, hurt his feet when he walked. They had done so ever since he had been born, but never had his feet been sticky so that the irritation continued with him for more than a single step.

Now he gazed upon his foot, and waited for the thought within him to develop. Meanwhile, he slowly removed the sharp-pointed fragments, one by one. Partly coated as they were with the half-liquid gum from his feet, they clung to his fingers as they had to his feet, except upon those portions where the oil was thick as before.

Burl's reasoning, before, was simple and of the primary order. Where oil covered him, the web did not. Therefore he would coat the rest of himself with oil. Had he been placed in the same predicament again, he would have used the same means of escape. But to apply a bit of knowledge gained in one predicament to another difficulty was something he had not yet done.

A dog may be taught that by pulling on the latchstring of a door he may open it, but the same dog coming to a high and close-barred gate with a latchstring attached, will never think of pulling on this second latchstring. He associates a latchstring with the opening of the door. The opening of a gate is another matter entirely.

Burl had been stirred to one invention by imminent peril. That is not extraordinary. But to reason in cold blood, as he presently did, that oil on his feet would nullify the glue upon his feet and enable him again to walk in comfort—that was a triumph. The inventions of savages are essentially matters of life and death, of food and safety. Comfort and luxury are only produced by intelligence of a high order.

Burl, in safety, had added to his comfort. That was truly a more important thing in his development than almost any other thing he could have done. He oiled his feet.

It was an almost infinitesimal problem, but Burl's struggles with the mental process of reasoning were actual. Thirty thousand years before him, a wise man had pointed out that education is simply training in thought, in efficient and effective thinking. Burl's tribe had been too much preoccupied with food and mere existence to think, and now Burl, sitting at the base of a squat toadstool that all but concealed him, reexemplified Rodin's "Thinker" for the first time in many generations.

For Burl to reason that oil upon the soles of his feet would guard him against sharp stones was as much a triumph of intellect as any masterpiece of art in the ages before him. Burl was learning how to think.

He stood up, walked, and crowed in sheer delight, then paused a moment in awe of his own intelligence. Thirty-five miles from his tribe, naked, unarmed, utterly ignorant of fire, of wood, of any weapons save a spear he had experimented with the day before, abysmally uninformed concerning the very existence of any art or science, Burl stopped to assure himself that he was very wonderful.

Pride came to him. He wished to display himself to Saya, these things upon his feet, and his spear. But his spear was gone.

*

With touching faith in the efficacy of this new pastime, Burl sat promptly down again and knitted his brows. Just as a superstitious person, once convinced that by appeal to a favorite talisman he will be guided aright, will inevitably apply to that talisman on all occasions, so Burl plumped himself down to think.

These questions were easily answered. Burl was naked. He would search out garments for himself. He was weaponless. He would find himself a spear. He was hungry—and would seek food, and he was far from his tribe, so he would go to them. Puerile reasoning, of course, but valuable, because it was consciously reasoning, consciously appealing to his mind for guidance in difficulty, deliberate progress from a mental desire to a mental resolution.

Even in the high civilization of ages before, few men had really used their brains. The great majority of people had depended upon machines and their leaders to think for them. Burl's tribefolk depended on their stomachs. Burl, however, was gradually developing the habit of thinking which makes for leadership and which would be invaluable to his little tribe.

He stood up again and faced upstream, moving slowly and cautiously, his eyes searching the ground before him keenly and his ears alert for the slightest sound of danger. Gigantic butterflies, riotous in coloring, fluttered overhead through the misty haze. Sometimes a grasshopper hurtled through the air like a projectile, its transparent wings beating the air frantically. Now and then a wasp sped by, intent upon its hunting, or a bee droned heavily along, anxious and worried, striving in a nearly flowerless world to gather the pollen that would feed the hive.

Here and there Burl saw flies of various sorts, some no larger than his thumb, but others the size of his whole hand. They fed upon the juices that dripped from the maggot-infested mushrooms, when filth more to their liking was not at hand.

Very far away a shrill roaring sounded faintly. It was like a multitude of clickings blended into a single sound, but was so far away that it did not impress itself upon Burl's attention. He had all the strictly localized vision of a child. What was near was important, and what was distant could be ignored. Only the imminent required attention, and Burl was preoccupied.

Had he listened, he would have realized that army ants were abroad in countless millions, spreading themselves out in a broad array and eating all they came upon far more destructively than so many locusts.

Locusts in past ages had eaten all green things. There were only giant cabbages and a few such tenacious rank growths in the world that Burl knew. The locusts had vanished with civilization and knowledge and the greater part of mankind, but the army ants remained as an invincible enemy to men and insects, and the most of the fungus growths that covered the earth.

Burl did not notice the sound, however. He moved forward, briskly though cautiously, searching with his eyes for garments, food, and weapons. He confidently expected to find all of them within a short distance.

Surely enough he found a thicket—if one might call it so—of edible fungi no more than half a mile beyond the spot where he had improvised his sandals to protect the soles of his feet.

Without especial elation, Burl tugged at the largest until he had broken off a food supply for several days. He went on, eating as he did so, past a broad plain a mile and more across, being broken into odd little hillocks by gradually ripening and suddenly developing mushrooms with which he was unfamiliar.

The earth seemed to be in process of being pushed aside by rounded protuberances of which only the tips showed. Blood-red hemispheres seemed to be forcing aside the earth so they might reach the outer air.

Burl looked at them curiously, and passed among them without touching them. They were strange, and to him most strange things meant danger. In any event, he was full of a new purpose now. He wished garments and weapons.

Above the plain a wasp hovered, a heavy object dangling beneath its black belly, ornamented by a single red band. It was a wasp—the hairy sand-wasp—and it was bringing a paralyzed gray caterpillar to its burrow.

Burl watched it drop down with the speed and sureness of an arrow, pull aside a heavy, flat stone, and descend into the ground. It had a vertical shaft dug down for forty feet or more.

It descended, evidently inspected the interior, reappeared, and vanished into the hole again, dragging the gray worm after it. Burl, marching on over the broad plain that seemed stricken with some erupting disease from the number of red pimples making their appearance, did not know what passed below, but observed the wasp emerge again and busily scratch dirt and stones into the shaft until it was full.

The wasp had paralyzed a caterpillar, taken it to the already prepared burrow, laid an egg upon it, and rilled up the entrance. In course of time the egg would hatch into a grub barely as long as Burl's forefinger, which would then feed upon the torpid caterpillar until it had waxed large and fat. Then it would weave itself a chrysalis and sleep a long sleep, only to wake as a wasp and dig its way to the open air.

PLANET NIGHTMARE

Burl reached the farther side of the plain and found himself threading the aisles of one of the fungus forests in which the growths were hideous, misshapen travesties upon the trees they had supplanted. Bloated, yellow limbs branched off from rounded, swollen trunks. Here and there a pear-shaped puff-ball, Burl's height and half as much again, waited craftily until a chance touch should cause it to shoot upward a curling puff of infinitely fine dust.

Burl went cautiously. There were dangers here, but he moved forward steadily, none the less. A great mass of edible mushroom was slung under one of his arms, and from time to time he broke off a fragment and ate of it, while his large eyes searched this way and that for threats of harm.

Behind him, a high, shrill roaring had grown slightly in volume and nearness, but was still too far away to impress Burl. The army ants were working havoc in the distance. By thousands and millions, myriads upon myriads, they were foraging the country, clambering upon every eminence, descending into every depression, their antennae waving restlessly and their mandibles forever threateningly extended. The ground was black with them, each was ten inches and more in length.

A single such creature would be formidable to an unarmed and naked man like Burl, whose wisest move would be flight, but in their thousands and millions they presented a menace from which no escape seemed possible. They were advancing steadily and rapidly, shrill stridulations and a multitude of clickings marking their movements.

The great helpless caterpillars upon the giant cabbages heard the sound of their coming, but were too stupid to flee. The black multitudes covered the rank vegetables, and tiny but voracious jaws began to tear at the flaccid masses of flesh.

Each creature had some futile means of struggling. The caterpillars strove to throw off their innumerable assailants by writhings and contortions, wholly ineffective. The bees fought their entrance to the gigantic hives with stings and wingbeats. The moths took to the air in helpless blindness when discovered by the relentless throngs of small black insects which reeked of formic acid and left the ground behind them denuded in every living thing.

Before the oncoming horde was a world of teeming life, where mushrooms and fungi fought with thinning numbers of giant cabbages for

34

foothold. Behind the black multitude was—nothing. Mushrooms, cabbages, bees, wasps, crickets. Every creeping and crawling thing that did not get aloft before the black tide reached it was lost, torn to bits by tiny mandibles. Even the hunting spiders and tarantulas fell before the host of insects, having killed many in their final struggles, but overwhelmed by sheer numbers. And the wounded and dying army ants made food for their sound comrades.

There is no mercy among insects. Only the web-spiders sat unmoved and immovable in their colossal snares, secure in the knowledge that their gummy webs would discourage attempts at invasion along the slender supporting cables.

Surging onward, flowing like a monstrous, murky tide over the yellow, steaming earth, the army ants advanced. Their vanguard reached the river, and recoiled. Burl was perhaps five miles distant when they changed their course, communicating the altered line of march to those behind them in some mysterious fashion of transmitting intelligence.

Thirty thousand years before, scientists had debated gravely over the means of communication among ants. They had observed that a single ant finding a bit of booty too large for him to handle alone would return to the ant-city and return with others. From that one instance they deduced a language of gestures made with the antennae.

Burl had no wise theories. He merely knew facts, but he knew that the ants had some form of speech or transmission of ideas. Now, however, he was moving cautiously along toward the stamping grounds of his tribe, in complete ignorance of the black blanket of living creatures creeping over the ground toward him.

A million tragedies marked the progress of the insect army. There was a tiny colony of mining bees—Zebra bees—a single mother, some four feet long, had dug a huge gallery with some ten cells, in which she laid her eggs and fed her grubs with hard-gathered pollen. The grubs had waxed fat and large, became bees, and laid eggs in their turn, within the gallery their mother had dug out for them.

Ten such bulky insects now foraged busily for grubs within the ancestral home, while the founder of the colony had grown draggled and wingless with the passing of time. Unable to forage herself, the old bee became the guardian of the nest or hive, as is the custom among the mining bees. She closed the opening of the hive with her head, making a living barrier within the entrance, and withdrawing to give entrance and exit only to duly authenticated members of the extensive colony.

The ancient and draggled concierge of the underground dwelling was at her post when the wave of army ants swept over her. Tiny, evil-smelling feet trampled upon her. She emerged to fight with mandible and sting for the sanctity of the hive. In a moment she was a shaggy mass of biting ants, rending and tearing at her chitinous armour. The old bee fought madly, viciously, sounding a buzzing alarm to the colonists yet within the hive. They emerged, fighting as they came, for the gallery leading down was a dark flood of small insects.

*

For a few moments a battle such as would make an epic was in progress. Ten huge bees, each four to five feet long, fighting with legs and jaw, wing and mandible, with all the ferocity of as many tigers. The tiny, vicious ants covered them, snapping at their multiple eyes, biting at the tender joints in their armour—sometimes releasing the larger prey to leap upon an injured comrade wounded by the huge creature they battled in common.

The fight, however, could have but one ending. Struggle as the bees might, herculean as their efforts might be, they were powerless against the incredible numbers of their assailants, who tore them into tiny fragments and devoured them. Before the last shred of the hive's defenders had vanished, the hive itself was gutted alike of the grubs it had contained and the food brought to the grubs by such weary effort of the mature bees.

The army ants went on. Only an empty gallery remained, that and a few fragments of tough armour, unappetizing even to the omniverous ants.

Burl was meditatively inspecting the scene of a recent tragedy, where rent and scraped fragments of a great beetle's shiny casing lay upon the ground. A greater beetle had come upon the first and slain him. Burl was looking upon the remains of the meal.

Three or four minims, little ants barely six inches long, foraged industriously among the bits. A new ant city was to be formed and the queen-ant lay hidden a half-mile away. These were the first hatchlings, who would feed the larger ants on whom would fall the great work of the ant-city. Burl ignored them, searching with his eyes for a spear or weapon.

MURRAY LEINSTER

Behind him the clicking roar, the high-pitched stridulations of the horde of army ants, rose in volume. Burl turned disgustedly away. The best he could find in the way of a weapon was a fiercely toothed hind leg. He picked it up, and an angry whine rose from the ground.

One of the black minims was working busily to detach a fragment of flesh from the joint of the leg, and Burl had snatched the morsel from him. The little creature was hardly half a foot in length, but it advanced upon Burl, shrilling angrily. He struck it with the leg and crushed it. Two of the other minims appeared, attracted by the noise the first had made. Discovering the crushed body of their fellow, they unceremoniously dismembered it and bore it away in triumph.

Burl went on, swinging the toothed limb in his hand. It made a fair club, and Burl was accustomed to use stones to crush the juicy legs of such giant crickets as his tribe sometimes came upon. He formed a half-defined idea of a club. The sharp teeth of the thing in his hand made him realize that a sidewise blow was better than a spearlike thrust.

The sound behind him had become a distant whispering, high-pitched, and growing nearer. The army ants swept over a mushroom forest, and the yellow, umbrella-like growths swarmed with black creatures devouring the substance on which they found a foothold.

A great bluebottle fly, shining with a metallic luster, reposed in an ecstasy of feasting, sipping through its long proboscis the dark-colored liquid that dripped slowly from a mushroom. Maggots filled the mushroom, and exuded a solvent pepsin that liquefied the white firm "meat."

They fed upon this soup, this gruel, and a surplus dripped to the ground below, where the bluebottle drank eagerly. Burl drew near, and struck. The fly collapsed into a writhing heap. Burl stood over it for an instant, pondering.

The army ants came nearer, down into a tiny valley, swarming into and through a little brook over which Burl had leaped. Ants can remain under water for a long time without drowning, so the small stream was but a minor obstacle, though the current of water swept many of them off their feet until they choked the brook-bed, and their comrades passed over their struggling bodies dry-shod. They were no more than temporarily annoyed, however, and presently crawled out to resume their march.

37

PLANET NIGHTMARE

About a quarter of a mile to the left of Burl's line of march, and perhaps a mile behind the spot where he stood over the dead bluebottle fly, there was a stretch of an acre or more where the giant, rank cabbages had so far resisted the encroachments of the ever present mushrooms. The pale, cross-shaped flowers of the cabbages formed food for many bees, and the leaves fed numberless grubs and worms, and loud-voiced crickets which crouched about on the ground, munching busily at the succulent green stuff. The army ants swept into the green area, ceaselessly devouring all they came upon.

A terrific din arose. The crickets hurtled away in a rocketlike flight, in a dark cloud of wildly beating wings. They shot aimlessly in any direction, with the result that half, or more than half, fell in the midst of the black tide of devouring insects and were seized as they fell. They uttered terrible cries as they were being torn to bits. Horrible inhuman screams reached Burl's ears.

A single such cry of agony would not have attracted Burl's attention—he lived in the very atmosphere of tragedy—but the chorus of creatures in torment made him look up. This was no minor horror. Wholesale slaughter was going on. He peered anxiously in the direction of the sound.

A wild stretch of sickly yellow fungus, here and there interspersed with a squat toadstool or a splash of vivid color where one of the many "rusts" had found a foothold. To the left a group of awkward, misshapen fungoids clustered in silent mockery of a forest of trees. There a mass of faded green, where the giant cabbages stood.

With the true sun never shining upon them save through a blanket of thick haze or heavy clouds, they were pallid things, but they were the only green things Burl had seen. Their nodding white flowers with four petals in the form of a cross glowed against the yellowish green leaves. But as Burl gazed toward them, the green became slowly black.

From where he stood, Burl could see two or three great grubs in lazy contentment, eating ceaselessly on the cabbages on which they rested. Suddenly first one and then the other began to jerk spasmodically. Burl saw that about each of them a tiny rim of black had clustered. Tiny black motes milled over the green surfaces of the cabbages. The grubs became black, the cabbages became black. Horrible contortions of the writhing grubs told of the agonies they were enduring. Then a black wave appeared at the further edge of the stretch of the sickly yellow fungus, a glistening, living wave, that moved forward rapidly with the roar of clickings and a persistent overtone of shrill stridulations.

The hair rose upon Burl's head. He knew what this was! He knew all too well the meaning of that tide of shining bodies. With a gasp of terror, all his intellectual preoccupations forgotten, he turned and fled in ultimate panic. And the tide came slowly on after him.

*

He flung away the great mass of edible mushroom, but clung to his sharp-toothed club desperately, and darted through the tangled aisles of the little mushroom forest with a heedless disregard of the dangers that might await him there. Flies buzzed about him loudly, huge creatures, glittering with a metallic luster. Once he was struck upon the shoulder by the body of one of them, and his skin was torn by the swiftly vibrating wings of the insect, as long as Burl's hand.

Burl thrust it away and sped on. The oil with which he was partly covered had turned rancid, now, and the odor attracted them, connoisseurs of the fetid. They buzzed over his head, keeping pace even with his headlong flight.

A heavy weight settled upon his head, and in a moment was doubled. Two of the creatures had dropped upon his oily hair, to sip the rancid oil through their disgusting proboscises. Burl shook them off with his hand and ran madly on. His ears were keenly attuned to the sound of the army ants behind him, and it grew but little farther away.

The clicking roar continued, but began to be overshadowed by the buzzing of the flies. In Burl's time the flies had no great heaps of putrid matter in which to lay their eggs. The ants—busy scavengers—carted away the debris of the multitudinous tragedies of the insect world long before it could acquire the gamey flavor beloved by the fly maggots. Only in isolated spots were the flies really numerous, but there they clustered in clouds that darkened the sky.

Such a buzzing, whirling cloud surrounded the madly running figure of Burl. It seemed as though a miniature whirlwind kept pace with the little pink-skinned man, a whirlwind composed of winged bodies and multi-faceted eyes. He twirled his club before him, and almost every stroke was interrupted by an impact against a thinly armoured body which collapsed with a spurting of reddish liquid.

An agonizing pain as of a red-hot iron struck upon Burl's back. One of the stinging flies had thrust its sharp-tipped proboscis into Burl's flesh to suck the blood.

Burl uttered a cry and—ran full tilt into the thick stalk of a blackened and draggled toadstool. There was a curious crackling as of wet punk or brittle rotten wood. The toadstool collapsed upon itself with a strange splashing sound. Many flies had laid their eggs in the fungoid, and it was a teeming mass of corruption and ill-smelling liquid.

With the crash of the toadstool's "head" upon the ground, it fell into a dozen pieces, and the earth for yards around was spattered with a stinking liquid in which tiny, headless maggots twitched convulsively.

The buzzing of the flies took on a note of satisfaction, and they settled by hundreds about the edges of the ill-smelling pools, becoming lost in the ecstacy of feasting while Burl staggered to his feet and darted off again. This time he was but a minor attraction to the flies, and but one or two came near him. From every direction they were hurrying to the toadstool feast, to the banquet of horrible, liquefied fungus that lay spread upon the ground.

Burl ran on. He passed beneath the wide-spreading leaves of a giant cabbage. A great grasshopper crouched upon the ground, its tremendous jaws crunching the rank vegetation voraciously. Half a dozen great worms ate steadily from their resting-places among the leaves. One of them had slung itself beneath an overhanging leaf—which would have thatched a dozen homes for as many men—and was placidly anchoring itself in preparation for the spinning of a cocoon in which to sleep the sleep of metamorphosis.

A mile away, the great black tide of army ants was advancing relentlessly. The great cabbage, the huge grasshopper, and all the stupid caterpillars upon the wide leaves would soon be covered with the tiny biting insects. The cabbage would be reduced to a chewed and destroyed stump, the colossal, furry grubs would be torn into a myriad mouthfuls and devoured by the black army ants, and the grasshopper would strike out with terrific, unguided strength, crushing its assailants by blows of its powerful hind legs and bites of its great jaws. But it would die, making terrible sounds of torment as the vicious mandibles of the army ants found crevices in its armour.

The clicking roar of the ants' advance overshadowed all other sounds, now. Burl was running madly, breath coming in great gasps, his eyes wide with panic. Alone of all the world about him, he knew the danger behind. The insects he passed were going about their business with that terrifying efficiency found only in the insect world.

*

There is something strangely daunting in the actions of an insect. It moves so directly, with such uncanny precision, with such utter indifference to anything but the end in view. Cannibalism is a rule, almost without exception. The paralysis of prey, so it may remain alive and fresh—though in agony—for weeks on end, is a common practice. The eating piecemeal of still living victims is a matter of course.

Absolute mercilessness, utter callousness, incredible inhumanity beyond anything known in the animal world is the natural and commonplace practice of the insects. And these vast cruelties are performed by armoured, machine-like creatures with an abstraction and a routine air that suggests a horrible Nature behind them all.

Burl nearly stumbled upon a tragedy. He passed within a dozen yards of a space where a female dung-beetle was devouring the mate whose honeymoon had begun that same day and ended in that gruesome fashion. Hidden behind a clump of mushrooms, a great yellow-banded spider was coyly threatening a smaller male of her own species. He was discreetly ardent, but if he won the favor of the gruesome creature he was wooing, he would furnish an appetizing meal for her some time within twenty-four hours.

Burl's heart was pounding madly. The breath whistled in his nostrils—and behind him, the wave of army ants was drawing nearer. They came upon the feasting flies. Some took to the air and escaped, but others were too engrossed in their delicious meal. The twitching little maggots, stranded upon the earth by the scattering of their soupy broth, were torn in pieces. The flies who were seized vanished into tiny maws. The serried ranks of black insects went on.

The tiny clickings of their limbs, the perpetual challenges and cross-challenges of crossed antennae, the stridulations of the creatures, all combined to make a high-pitched but deafening din. Now and then another sound pierced the noises made by the ants themselves. A cricket, seized by a thousand tiny jaws, uttered cries of agony. The shrill note of the crickets had grown deeply bass with the increase in size of the organs that uttered it.

There was a strange contrast between the ground before the advancing horde and that immediately behind it. Before, a busy world, teeming with life. Butterflies floating overhead on lazy wings, grubs waxing fat and huge upon the giant cabbages, crickets eating, great spiders sitting quietly in their lairs waiting with invincible patience for prey to draw near their trap doors or fall into their webs, colossal beetles lumbering heavily through the mushroom forests, seeking food, making love in monstrous, tragic fashion.

And behind the wide belt of army ants—chaos. The edible mushrooms gone. The giant cabbages left as mere stumps of unappetizing pulp, the busy life of the insect world completely wiped out save for the flying creatures that fluttered helplessly over an utterly changed landscape. Here and there little bands of stragglers moved busily over the denuded earth, searching for some fragment of food that might conceivably have been overlooked by the main body.

Burl was putting forth his last ounce of strength. His limbs trembled, his breathing was agony, sweat stood out upon his forehead. He ran a little, naked man with the disjointed fragment of a huge insect's limb in his hand, running for his insignificant life, running as if his continued existence among the million tragedies of that single day were the purpose for which the whole of the universe had been created.

He sped across an open space a hundred yards across. A thicket of beautifully golden mushrooms (*Agaricus caesareus*) barred his way. Beyond the mushrooms a range of strangely colored hills began, purple and green and black and gold, melting into each other, branching off from each other, inextricably tangled.

They rose to a height of perhaps sixty or seventy feet, and above them a little grayish haze had gathered. There seemed to be a layer of tenuous vapor upon their surfaces, which slowly rose and coiled, and gathered into a tiny cloudlet above their tips.

The hills, themselves, were but masses of fungus, mushrooms and fungoids of every description, yeasts, "musts," and every form of fungus growth which had grown within itself and about itself until this great mass of strangely colored, spongy stuff had gathered in a mass that undulated unevenly across the level earth for miles.

Burl burst through the golden thicket and attacked the ascent. His feet sank into the spongy sides of the hillock. Panting, gasping, staggering from exhaustion, he made his way up the top. He plunged into a little valley on the farther side, up another slope. For perhaps ten minutes he forced himself on, then collapsed. He lay, unable to move further, in a little hollow, his sharp-toothed club still clasped in his hands. Above him, a bright yellow butterfly with a thirty-foot spread of wing, fluttered lightly.

He lay motionless, breathing in great gasps, his limbs stubbornly refusing to lift him.

*

The sound of the army ants continued to grow near. At last, above the crest of the last hillock he had surmounted, two tiny antennae appeared, then the black glistening head of an army ant, the forerunner of its horde. It moved deliberately forward, waving its antennae ceaselessly. It made its way toward Burl, tiny clickings coming from the movements of its limbs.

A little wisp of tenuous vapor swirled toward the ant, a wisp of the same vapor that had gathered above the whole range of hills as a thin, low cloud. It enveloped the insect—and the ant seemed to be attacked by a strange convulsion. Its legs moved aimlessly. It threw itself desperately about. If it had been an animal, Burl would have watched with wondering eyes while it coughed and gasped, but it was an insect breathing through air-holes in its abdomen. It writhed upon the spongy fungus growth across which it had been moving.

Burl, lying in an exhausted, panting heap upon the purple mass of fungus, was conscious of a strange sensation. His body felt strangely warm. He knew nothing of fire or the heat of the sun, and the only sensation of warmth he had ever known was that caused when the members of his tribe had huddled together in their hiding place when the damp chill of the night had touched their soft-skinned bodies. Then the heat of their breaths and their bodies had kept out the chill.

This heat that Burl now felt was a hotter, fiercer heat. He moved his body with a tremendous effort, and for a moment the fungus was cool and soft beneath him. Then, slowly, the sensation of heat began again, and increased until Burl's skin was red and inflamed from the irritation.

The thin and tenuous vapor, too, made Burl's lungs smart and his eyes water. He was breathing in great, choking gasps, but the period of rest—short as it was—had enabled him to rise and stagger on. He crawled painfully to the top of the slope, and looked back.

The hill-crest on which he stood was higher than any of those he had passed in his painful run, and he could see clearly the whole of the purple range. Where he was, he was near the farther edge of the range, which was here perhaps half a mile wide.

It was a ceaseless, undulating mass of hills and hollows, ridges and spurs, all of them colored, purple and brown and golden-yellow, deepest black and dingy white. And from the tips of most of the pointed hills little wisps of vapor rose up.

A thin, dark cloud had gathered overhead. Burl could look to the right and left, and see the hills fading into the distance, growing fainter as the haze above them seemed to grow thicker. He saw, too, the advancing cohorts of the army ants, creeping over the tangled mass of fungus growth. They seemed to be feeding as they went, upon the fungus that had gathered into these incredible monstrosities.

The hills were living. They were not upheavals of the ground, they were festering heaps of insanely growing, festering mushrooms and fungus. Upon most of them a purple mould had spread itself so that they seemed a range of purple hills, but here and there patches of other vivid colors showed, and there was a large hill whose whole side was a brilliant golden hue. Another had tiny bright red spots of a strange and malignant mushroom whose properties Burl did not know, scattered all over the purple with which it was covered.

Burl leaned heavily upon his club and watched dully. He could run no more. The army ants were spreading everywhere over the mass of fungus. They would reach him soon.

Far to the right the vapor thickened. A column of smoke arose. What Burl did not know and would never know was that far down in the interior of that compressed mass of fungus, slow oxidization had been going on. The temperature of the interior had been raised. In the darkness and the dampness deep down in the hills, spontaneous combustion had begun.

Just as the vast piles of coal the railroad companies of thirty thousand years before had gathered together sometimes began to burn fiercely in their interiors, and just as the farmers' piles of damp straw suddenly burst into fierce flames from no cause, so these huge piles of tinder-like mushrooms had been burning slowly within themselves.

There had been no flames, because the surface remained intact and nearly air-tight. But when the army ants began to tear at the edible surfaces despite the heat they encountered, fresh air found its way to the smouldering masses of fungus. The slow combustion became rapid combustion. The dull heat became fierce flames. The slow trickle of thin smoke became a huge column of thick, choking, acrid stuff that set the army ants that breathed it into spasms of convulsive writhing.

From a dozen points the flames burst out. A dozen or more columns of blinding smoke rose to the heavens. A pall of fume-laden smoke gathered above the range of purple hills, while Burl watched apathetically. And the serried ranks of army ants marched on to the widening furnaces that awaited them.

They had recoiled from the river, because their instinct had warned them. Thirty thousand years without danger from fire, however, had let their racial fear of fire die out. They marched into the blazing orifices they had opened in the hills, snapping with their mandibles at the leaping flames, springing at the glowing tinder.

*

The blazing area widened, as the purple surface was undermined and fell in. Burl watched the phenomenon without comprehension and even without thankfulness. He stood, panting more and more slowly, breathing more and more easily, until the glow from the approaching flames reddened his skin and the acrid smoke made tears flow from his eyes.

Then he retreated slowly, leaning on his club and looking back. The black wave of the army ants was sweeping into the fire, sweeping into the incredible heat of that carbonized material burning with an open flame. At last there were only the little bodies of stragglers from the great ant-army, scurrying here and there over the ground their comrades had denuded of all living things. The bodies of the main army had vanished—burnt to crisp ashes in the furnace of the hills.

PLANET NIGHTMARE

There had been agony in that flame, dreadful agony such as no man would like to dwell upon. The insane courage of the ants, attacking with their horny jaws the burning masses of fungus, rolling over and over with a flaming missile clutched in their mandibles, sounding their shrill war cry while cries of agony came from them—blinded, their antennae burnt off, their lidless eyes scorched by the licking flames, yet going madly forward on flaming feet to attack, ever attack this unknown and unknowable enemy.

Burl made his way slowly over the hills. Twice he saw small bodies of the army ants. They had passed between the widening surfaces their comrades had opened, and they were feeding voraciously upon the hills they trod on. Once Burl was spied, and a shrill war cry was sounded, but he moved on, and the ants were busily eating. A single ant rushed toward him. Burl brought down his club, and a writhing body remained to be eaten later by its comrades when they came upon it.

Again night fell. The skies grew red in the west, though the sun did not shine through the ever present cloud bank. Darkness spread across the sky. Utter blackness fell over the whole mad world, save where the luminous mushrooms shed their pale light upon the ground and fireflies the length of Burl's arm shed their fitful gleams upon an earth of fungus growths and monstrous insects.

Burl made his way across the range of mushroom hills, picking his path with his large blue eyes whose pupils expanded to great size. Slowly, from the sky, now a drop and then a drop, now a drop and then a drop, the nightly rain that would continue until daybreak began.

Burl found the ground hard beneath his feet. He listened keenly for sounds of danger. Something rustled heavily in a thicket of mushrooms a hundred yards away. There were sounds of preening, and of delicate feet placed lightly here and there upon the ground. Then the throbbing beat of huge wings began suddenly, and a body took to the air.

A fierce, down-coming current of air smote Burl, and he looked upward in time to catch the outline of a huge body—a moth—as it passed above him. He turned to watch the line of its flight, and saw a strange glow in the sky behind him. The mushroom hills were still burning.

He crouched beneath a squat toadstool and waited for the dawn, his club held tightly in his hands, and his ears alert for any sound of danger. The slow-dropping, sodden rain kept on. It fell with irregular, drumlike beats upon the tough top of the toadstool under which he had taken refuge.

Slowly, slowly, the sodden rainfall continued. Drop by drop, all the night long, the warm pellets of liquid came from the sky. They boomed upon the hollow heads of the toadstools, and splashed into the steaming pools that lay festering all over the fungus-covered earth.

And all the night long the great fires grew and spread in the mass of already half-carbonized mushroom. The flare at the horizon grew brighter and nearer. Burl, naked and hiding beneath a huge mushroom, watched it grow near him with wide eyes, wondering what this thing was. He had never seen a flame before.

The overhanging clouds were brightened by the flames. Over a stretch at least a dozen miles in length and from half a mile to three miles across, seething furnaces sent columns of dense smoke up to the roof of clouds, luminous from the glow below them, and spreading out and forming an intermediate layer below the cloudbanks.

It was like the glow of all the many lights of a vast city thrown against the sky—but the last great city had moulded into fungus-covered rubbish thirty thousand years before. Like the flitting of airplanes above a populous city, too, was the flitting of fascinated creatures above the glow.

*

Moths and great flying beetles, gigantic gnats and midges grown huge with the passing of time, they fluttered and danced the dance of death above the flames. As the fire grew nearer to Burl, he could see them.

Colossal, delicately formed creatures swooped above the strange blaze. Moths with their riotously colored wings of thirty-foot spread beat the air with mighty strokes, and their huge eyes glowed like carbuncles as they stared with the frenzied gaze of intoxicated devotees into the glowing flames below them.

Burl saw a great peacock moth soaring above the burning mushroom hills. Its wings were all of forty feet across, and fluttered like gigantic sails as the moth gazed down at the flaming furnace below. The separate flames had united, now, and a single sheet of white-hot burning stuff spread across the country for miles, sending up its clouds of smoke, in which and through which the fascinated creatures flew.

PLANET NIGHTMARE

Feathery antennae of the finest lace spread out before the head of the peacock moth, and its body was softest, richest velvet. A ring of snow-white down marked where its head began, and the red glow from below smote on the maroon of its body with a strange effect.

For one instant it was outlined clearly. Its eyes glowed more redly than any ruby's fire, and the great, delicate wings were poised in flight. Burl caught the flash of the flames upon two great iridescent spots upon the wide-spread wings. Shining purple and vivid red, the glow of opal and the sheen of pearl, all the glory of chalcedony and chrysoprase formed a single wonder in the red glare of burning fungus. White smoke compassed the great moth all about, dimming the radiance of its gorgeous dress.

Burl saw it dart straight into the thickest and brightest of the licking flames, flying madly, eagerly, into the searing, hellish heat as a willing, drunken sacrifice to the god of fire.

Monster flying beetles with their horny wing-cases stiffly stretched, blundered above the reeking, smoking pyre. In the red light from before them they shone like burnished metal, and their clumsy bodies with the spurred and fierce-toothed limbs darted like so many grotesque meteors through the luminous haze of ascending smoke.

Burl saw strange collisions and still stranger meetings. Male and female flying creatures circled and spun in the glare, dancing their dance of love and death in the wild radiance from the funeral pyre of the purple hills. They mounted higher than Burl could see, drunk with the ecstasy of living, then descended to plunge headlong to death in the roaring fires beneath them.

From every side the creatures came. Moths of brightest yellow with soft and furry bodies palpitant with life flew madly into the column of light that reached to the overhanging clouds, then moths of deepest black with gruesome symbols upon their wings came swiftly to dance, like motes in a bath of sunlight, above the glow.

And Burl sat crouched beneath an overshadowing toadstool and watched. The perpetual, slow, sodden raindrops fell. A continual faint hissing penetrated the sound of the fire—the raindrops being turned to steam. The air was alive with flying things. From far away, Burl heard a strange, deep bass muttering. He did not know the cause, but there was a vast swamp, of the existence of which he was ignorant, some ten or fifteen miles away, and the chorus of insect-eating giant frogs reached his ears even at that distance.

The night wore on, while the flying creatures above the fire danced and died, their numbers ever recruited by fresh arrivals. Burl sat tensely still, his wide eyes watching everything, his mind groping for an explanation of what he saw. At last the sky grew dimly gray, then brighter, and day came on. The flames of the burning hills grew faint as the fire died down, and after a long time Burl crept from his hiding place and stood erect.

A hundred yards from where he was, a straight wall of smoke rose from the still smouldering fungus, and Burl could see it stretching for miles in either direction. He turned to continue on his way, and saw the remains of one of the tragedies of the night.

A huge moth had flown into the flames, been horribly scorched, and floundered out again. Had it been able to fly, it would have returned to its devouring deity, but now it lay immovable upon the ground, its antennae seared hopelessly, one beautiful, delicate wing burned in gaping holes, its eyes dimmed by flame and its exquisitely tapering limbs broken and crushed by the force with which it had struck the ground. It lay helpless upon the earth, only the stumps of its antennae moving restlessly, and its abdomen pulsating slowly as it drew pain-racked breaths.

Burl drew near and picked up a stone. He moved on presently, a velvet cloak cast over his shoulders, gleaming with all the colors of the rainbow. A gorgeous mass of soft, blue moth fur was about his middle, and he had bound upon his forehead two yard-long, golden fragments of the moth's magnificent antennae. He strode on, slowly, clad as no man had been clad in all the ages.

After a little he secured a spear and took up his journey to Saya, looking like a prince of Ind upon a bridal journey—though no mere prince ever wore such raiment in days of greatest glory.

*

For many long miles Burl threaded his way through a single forest of thin-stalked toadstools. They towered three-man-heights high, and all about their bases were streaks and splashes of the rusts and moulds that preyed upon them. Twice Burl came to open glades wherein open, bubbling pools of green slime festered in corruption, and once he hid himself fearfully as a monster scarabeus beetle lumbered within three yards of him, moving heavily onward with a clanking of limbs as of some mighty machine.

Burl saw the mighty armour and the inward-curving jaws of the creature, and envied him his weapons. The time was not yet come, however, when Burl would smile at the great insect and hunt him for the juicy flesh contained in those armoured limbs.

Burl was still a savage, still ignorant, still timid. His principal advance had been that whereas he had fled without reasoning, he now paused to see if he need flee. In his hands he bore a long, sharp-pointed chitinous spear. It had been the weapon of a huge, unnamed flying insect scorched to death in the burning of the purple hills, which had floundered out of the flames to die. Burl had worked for an hour before being able to detach the weapon he coveted. It was as long and longer than Burl himself.

He was a strange sight, moving slowly and cautiously through the shadowed lanes of the mushroom forest. A cloak of delicate velvet in which all the colors of the rainbow played in iridescent beauty hung from his shoulders. A mass of soft and beautiful moth fur was about his middle, and in the strip of sinew about his waist the fiercely toothed limb of a fighting beetle was thrust carelessly. He had bound to his forehead twin stalks of a great moth's feathery golden antennae.

Against the play of color that came from his borrowed plumage his pink skin showed in odd contrast. He looked like some proud knight walking slowly through the gardens of a goblin's castle. But he was still a fearful creature, no more than the monstrous creatures about him save in the possession of latent intelligence. He was weak—and therein lay his greatest promise. A hundred thousand years before him his ancestors had been forced by lack of claws and fangs to develop brains.

Burl was sunk as low as they had been, but he had to combat more horrifying enemies, more inexorable threatenings, and many times more crafty assailants. His ancestors had invented knives and spears and flying missiles. The creatures about Burl had knives and spears a thousand times more deadly than the weapons that had made his ancestors masters of the woods and forests.

Burl was in comparison vastly more weak than his forebears had been, and it was that weakness that in times to come would lead him and those who followed him to heights his ancestors had never known. But now—

He heard a discordant, deep bass bellow, coming from a spot not twenty yards away. In a flash of panic he darted behind a clump of mushrooms and hid himself, panting in sheer terror. He waited for an instant in frozen fear, motionless and tense. His wide, blue eyes were glassy.

The bellow came again, but this time with a querulous note. Burl heard a crashing and plunging as of some creature caught in a snare. A mushroom fell with a brittle snapping, and the spongy thud as it fell to the ground was followed by a tremendous commotion. Something was fighting desperately against something else, but Burl did not know what creature or creatures might be in combat.

He waited for a long time, and the noise gradually died away. Presently Burl's breath came more slowly, and his courage returned. He stole from his hiding place, and would have made away, but something held him back. Instead of creeping from the scene, he crept cautiously over toward the source of the noise.

He peered between two cream-colored toadstool stalks and saw the cause of the noise. A wide, funnel-shaped snare of silk was spread out before him, some twenty yards across and as many deep. The individual threads could be plainly seen, but in the mass it seemed a fabric of sheerest, finest texture. Held up by the tall mushrooms, it was anchored to the ground below, and drew away to a tiny point through which a hole gave on some yet unknown recess. And all the space of the wide snare was hung with threads, fine, twisted threads no more than half the thickness of Burl's finger.

This was the trap of a labyrinth spider. Not one of the interlacing threads was strong enough to hold the feeblest of prey, but the threads were there by thousands. A great cricket had become entangled in the maze of sticky lines. Its limbs thrashed out, smashing the snare-lines at every stroke, but at every stroke meeting and becoming entangled with a dozen more. It thrashed about mightily, emitting at intervals the horrible, deep bass cry that the chirping voice of the cricket had become with its increase in size.

*

Burl breathed more easily, and watched with a fascinated curiosity. Mere death—even tragic death—as among insects held no great interest for him. It was a matter of such common and matter-of-fact occurrence that he was not greatly stirred. But a spider and his prey was another matter.

51

PLANET NIGHTMARE

There were few insects that deliberately sought man. Most insects have their allotted victims, and will touch no others, but spiders have a terrifying impartiality. One great beetle devouring another was a matter of indifference to Burl. A spider devouring some luckless insect was but an example of what might happen to him. He watched alertly, his gaze traveling from the enmeshed cricket to the strange orifice at the rear of the funnel-shaped snare.

The opening darkened. Two shining, glistening eyes had been watching from the rear of the funnel. It drew itself into a tunnel there, in which the spider had been waiting. Now it swung out lightly and came toward the cricket. It was a gray spider (*Agelena labyrinthica*), with twin black ribbons upon its thorax, next the head, and with two stripes of curiously speckled brown and white upon its abdomen. Burl saw, too, two curious appendages like a tail.

It came nimbly out of its tunnel-like hiding place and approached the cricket. The cricket was struggling only feebly now, and the cries it uttered were but feeble, because of the confining threads that fettered its limbs. Burl saw the spider throw itself upon the cricket and saw the final, convulsive shudder of the insect as the spider's fangs pierced its tough armour. The sting lasted a long time, and finally Burl saw that the spider was really feeding. All the succulent juices of the now dead cricket were being sucked from its body by the spider. It had stung the cricket upon the haunch, and presently it went to the other leg and drained that, too, by means of its powerful internal suction-pump. When the second haunch had been sucked dry, the spider pawed the lifeless creature for a few moments and left it.

Food was plentiful, and the spider could afford to be dainty in its feeding. The two choicest titbits had been consumed. The remainder could be discarded.

A sudden thought came to Burl and quite took his breath away. For a second his knees knocked together in self-induced panic. He watched the gray spider carefully with growing determination in his eyes. He, Burl, had killed a hunting-spider upon the red-clay cliff. True, the killing had been an accident, and had nearly cost him his own life a few minutes later in the web-spider's snare, but he had killed a spider, and of the most deadly kind.

MURRAY LEINSTER

Now, a great ambition was growing in Burl's heart. His tribe had always feared spiders too much to know much of their habits, but they knew one or two things. The most important was that the snare-spiders never left their lairs to hunt—never! Burl was about to make a daring application of that knowledge.

He drew back from the white and shining snare and crept softly to the rear. The fabric gathered itself into a point and then continued for some twenty feet as a tunnel, in which the spider waited while dreaming of its last meal and waiting for the next victim to become entangled in the labyrinth in front. Burl made his way to a point where the tunnel was no more than ten feet away, and waited.

Presently, through the interstices of the silk, he saw the gray bulk of the spider. It had left the exhausted body of the cricket, and returned to its resting place. It settled itself carefully upon the soft walls of the tunnel, with its shining eyes fixed upon the tortuous threads of its trap. Burl's hair was standing straight up upon his head from sheer fright, but he was the slave of an idea.

He drew near and poised his spear, his new and sharp spear, taken from the body of an unknown flying creature killed by the burning purple hills. Burl raised the spear and aimed its sharp and deadly point at the thick gray bulk he could see dimly through the threads of the tunnel. He thrust it home with all his strength—and ran away at the top of his speed, glassy-eyed from terror.

A long time later he ventured near again, his heart in his mouth, ready to flee at the slightest sound. All was still. Burl had missed the horrible convulsions of the wounded spider, had not heard the frightful gnashings of its fangs as it tore at the piercing weapon, had not seen the silken threads of the tunnel ripped as the spider—hurt to death—had struggled with insane strength to free itself.

He came back beneath the overshadowing toadstools, stepping quietly and cautiously, to find a great rent in the silken tunnel, to find the great gray bulk lifeless and still, half-fallen through the opening the spear had first made. A little puddle of evil-smelling liquid lay upon the ground below the body, and from time to time a droplet fell from the spear into the puddle with a curious splash.

PLANET NIGHTMARE

Burl looked at what he had done, saw the dead body of the creature he had slain, saw the ferocious mandibles, and the keen and deadly fangs. The dead eyes of the creature still stared at him malignantly, and the hairy legs were still braced as if further to enlarge the gaping hole through which it had partly fallen.

Exultation filled Burl's heart. His tribe had been but furtive vermin for thousands of years, fleeing from the mighty insects, hiding from them, and if overtaken but waiting helplessly for death, screaming shrilly in terror.

He, Burl, had turned the tables. He had slain one of the enemies of his tribe. His breast expanded. Always his tribesmen went quietly and fearfully, making no sound. But a sudden, exultant yell burst from Burl's lips—the first hunting cry from the lips of a man in three hundred centuries!

*

The next second his pulse nearly stopped in sheer panic at having made such a noise. He listened fearfully, but there was no sound. He drew near his prey and carefully withdrew his spear. The viscid liquid made it slimy and slippery, and he had to wipe it dry against a leathery toadstool. Then Burl had to conquer his illogical fear again before daring to touch the creature he had slain.

He moved off presently, with the belly of the spider upon his back and two of the hairy legs over his shoulders. The other limbs of the monster hung limp, and trailed upon the ground. Burl was now a still more curious sight as a gayly colored object with a cloak shining in iridescent colors, the golden antennae of a great moth rising from his forehead, and the hideous bulk of a gray spider for a burden.

He moved through the thin-stalked mushroom forest, and, because of the thing he carried, all creatures fled before him. They did not fear man—their instinct was slow-moving—but during all the millions of years that insects have existed, there have existed spiders to prey upon them. So Burl moved on in solemn state, a brightly clad man bent beneath the weight of a huge and horrible monster.

He came upon a valley full of torn and blackened mushrooms. There was not a single yellow top among them. Every one had been infested with tiny maggots which had liquefied the tough meat of the mushroom and caused it to drip to the ground below. And all the liquid had gathered in a golden pool in the center of the small depression. Burl heard a loud humming and buzzing before he topped the rise that opened the valley for his inspection. He stopped a moment and looked down.

A golden-red lake, its center reflecting the hazy sky overhead. All about, blackened mushrooms, seeming to have been charred and burned by a fierce flame. A slow-flowing golden brooklet trickled slowly over a rocky ledge, into the larger pool. And all about the edges of the golden lake, in ranks and rows, by hundreds, thousands, and by millions, were ranged the green-gold, shining bodies of great flies.

They were small as compared with the other insects. They had increased in size but a fraction of the amount that the bees, for example, had increased; but it was due to an imperative necessity of their race.

The flesh-flies laid their eggs by hundreds in decaying carcases. The others laid their eggs by hundreds in the mushrooms. To feed the maggots that would hatch, a relatively great quantity of food was needed, therefore the flies must remain comparatively small, or the body of a single grasshopper, say, would furnish food for but two or three grubs instead of the hundreds it must support.

Burl stared down at the golden pool. Bluebottles, greenbottles, and all the flies of metallic luster were gathered at the Lucullan feast of corruption. Their buzzing as they darted above the odorous pool of golden liquid made the sound Burl had heard. Their bodies flashed and glittered as they darted back and forth, seeking a place to alight and join in the orgy.

Those which clustered about the banks of the pool were still as if carved from metal. Their huge, red eyes glowed, and their bodies shone with an obscene fatness. Flies are the most disgusting of all insects. Burl watched them a moment, watched the interlacing streams of light as they buzzed eagerly above the pool, seeking a place at the festive board.

A drumming roar sounded in the air. A golden speck appeared in the sky, a slender, needle-like body with transparent, shining wings and two huge eyes. It grew nearer and became a dragonfly twenty feet and more in length, its body shimmering, purest gold. It poised itself above the pool and then darted down. Its jaws snapped viciously and repeatedly, and at each snapping the glittering body of a fly vanished.

A second dragonfly appeared, its body a vivid purple, and a third. They swooped and rushed above the golden pool, snapping in mid air, turning their abrupt, angular turns, creatures of incredible ferocity and beauty. At the moment they were nothing more or less than slaughtering-machines. They darted here and there, their many-faceted eyes burning with blood-lust. In that mass of buzzing flies even the most voracious appetite must be sated, but the dragonflies kept on. Beautiful, slender, graceful creatures, they dashed here and there above the pond like avenging fiends or the mythical dragons for which they had been named.

*

Only a few miles farther on Burl came upon a familiar landmark. He knew it well, but from a safe distance as always. A mass of rock had heaved itself up from the nearly level plain over which he was traveling, and formed an outjutting cliff. At one point the rock overhung a sheer drop, making an inverted ledge—a roof over nothingness—which had been pre-empted by a hairy creature and made into a fairylike dwelling. A white hemisphere clung tenaciously to the rock above, and long cables anchored it firmly.

Burl knew the place as one to be fearfully avoided. A Clotho spider (*Clotho Durandi, LATR*) had built itself a nest there, from which it emerged to hunt the unwary. Within that half-globe there was a monster, resting upon a cushion of softest silk. But if one went too near, one of the little inverted arches, seemingly firmly closed by a wall of silk, would open and a creature out of a dream of hell emerge, to run with fiendish agility toward its prey.

Surely, Burl knew the place. Hung upon the outer walls of the silken palace were stones and tiny boulders, discarded fragments of former meals, and the gutted armour from limbs of ancient prey. But what caused Burl to know the place most surely and most terribly was another decoration that dangled from the castle of this insect ogre. This was the shrunken, desiccated figure of a man, all its juices extracted and the life gone.

The death of that man had saved Burl's life two years before. They had been together, seeking a new source of edible mushrooms for food. The Clotho spider was a hunter, not a spinner of snares. It sprang suddenly from behind a great puff-ball, and the two men froze in terror. Then it came swiftly forward and deliberately chose its victim. Burl had escaped when the other man was seized. Now he looked meditatively at the hiding place of his ancient enemy. Some day—

56

But now he passed on. He went past the thicket in which the great moths hid during the day, and past the pool—a turgid thing of slime and yeast—in which a monster water snake lurked. He penetrated the little wood of the shining mushrooms that gave out light at night, and the shadowed place where the truffle-hunting beetles went chirping thunderously during the dark hours.

And then he saw Saya. He caught a flash of pink skin vanishing behind the thick stalk of a squat toadstool, and ran forward, calling her name. She appeared, and saw the figure with the horrible bulk of the spider upon its back. She cried out in horror, and Burl understood. He let his burden fall and then went swiftly toward her.

They met. Saya waited timidly until she saw who this man was, and then astonishment went over her face. Gorgeously attired, in an iridescent cloak from the whole wing of a great moth, with a strip of softest fur from a night-flying creature about his middle, with golden, feathery antennae bound upon his forehead, and a fierce spear in his hands—this was not the Burl she had known.

But then he moved slowly toward her, filled with a fierce delight at seeing her again, thrilling with joy at the slender gracefulness of her form and the dark richness of her tangled hair. He held out his hands and touched her shyly. Then, manlike, he began to babble excitedly of the things that had happened to him, and dragged her toward his great victim, the gray-bellied spider.

Saya trembled when she saw the furry bulk lying upon the ground, and would have fled when Burl advanced and took it upon his back. Then something of the pride that filled him came vicariously to her. She smiled a flashing smile, and Burl stopped short in his excited explanation. He was suddenly tongue-tied. His eyes became pleading and soft. He laid the huge spider at her feet and spread out his hands imploringly.

Thirty thousand years of savagery had not lessened the femininity in Saya. She became aware that Burl was her slave, that these wonderful things he wore and had done were as nothing if she did not approve. She drew away—saw the misery in Burl's face—and abruptly ran into his arms and clung to him, laughing happily. And quite suddenly Burl saw with extreme clarity that all these things he had done, even the slaying of a great spider, were of no importance whatever beside this most wonderful thing that had just happened, and told Saya so quite humbly, but holding her very close to him as he did so.

And so Burl came back to his tribe. He had left it nearly naked, with but a wisp of moth-wing twisted about his middle, a timid, fearful, trembling creature. He returned in triumph, walking slowly and fearlessly down a broad lane of golden mushrooms toward the hiding place of his people.

Upon his shoulders was draped a great and many-colored cloak made from the whole of a moth's wing. Soft fur was about his middle. A spear was in his hand and a fierce club at his waist. He and Saya bore between them the dead body of a huge spider—aforetime the dread of the pink-skinned, naked men. But to Burl the most important thing of all was that Saya walked beside him openly, acknowledging him before all the tribe.

THE RED DUST

PREY

The sky grew gray and then almost white. The overhanging banks of clouds seemed to withdraw a little from the steaming earth. Haze that hung always among the mushroom forests and above the fungus hills grew more tenuous, and the slow and misty rain that dripped the whole night long ceased reluctantly.

As far as the eye could see a mad world stretched out, a world of insensate cruelties and strange, fierce maternal solicitudes. The insects of the night—the great moths whose wings spread far and wide in the dimness, and the huge fireflies, four feet in length, whose beacons made the earth glow in their pale, weird light—the insects of the night had sought their hiding-places.

Now the creatures of the day ventured forth. A great ant-hill towered a hundred feet in the air. Upon its gravel and boulder-strewn side a commotion became visible.

The earth crumbled, and fell into an invisible opening, then a dark chasm appeared, and two slender, threadlike antennæ peered out.

A warrior ant emerged, and stood for an instant in the daylight, looking all about for signs of danger to the ant-city. He was all of ten inches long, this ant, and his mandibles were fierce and strong. A second and third warrior came from the inside of the ant-hill, and ran with tiny clickings about the hillock, waving their antennæ restlessly, searching, ever searching for a menace to their city.

They returned to the gateway from which they had made their appearance, evidently bearing reassuring messages, because shortly after they had reëntered the gateway of the ant-city, a flood of black, ill-smelling workers poured out of the opening and dispersed upon their business. The clickings of their limbs and an occasional whining stridulation made an incessant sound as they scattered over the earth, foraging among the mushrooms and giant cabbages, among the rubbish-heaps of the gigantic bee-hives and wasp colonies, and among the remains of the tragedies of the night for food for their city.

The city of the ants had begun its daily toil, toil in which every one shared without supervision or coercion. Deep in the recesses of the pyramid galleries were hollowed out and winding passages that led down a fathomless distance into the earth below.

Somewhere in the maze of tunnels there was a royal apartment, in which the queen-ant reposed, waited upon by assiduous courtiers, fed by royal stewards, and combed and rubbed by the hands of her subjects and children.

But even the huge monarch of the city had her constant and pressing duty of maternity. A dozen times the size of her largest loyal servant, she was no less bound by the unwritten but imperative laws of the city than they. From the time of waking to the time of rest, she was ordained to be the queen-mother in the strictest and most literal sense of the word, for at intervals to be measured only in terms of minutes she brought forth a single egg, perhaps three inches in length, which was instantly seized by one of her eager attendants and carried in haste to the municipal nursery.

There it was placed in a tiny cell a foot or more in length until a sac-shaped grub appeared, all soft, white body save for a tiny mouth. Then the nurses took it in charge and fed it with curious, tender gestures until it had waxed large and fat and slept the sleep of metamorphosis. When it emerged from its rudimentary cocoon it took the places of its nurses until its soft skin had hardened into the horny armor of the workers and soldiers, and then it joined the throng of workers that poured out from the city at dawn to forage for food, to bring back its finds and to share with the warriors and the nurses, the drone males and the young queens, and all the other members of its communities, their duties in the city itself. That was the life of the social insect, absolute devotion to the cause of its city, utter abnegation of self-interest for the sake of its fellows—and death at their hands when their usefulness was past. They neither knew nor expected more or less.

It is a strange instinct that prompts these creatures to devote their lives to their city, taking no smallest thought for their individual good, without even the call of maternity or sex to guide them. Only the queen knows motherhood. The others know nothing but toil, for purposes they do not understand, and to an end of which they cannot dream. At intervals all over the world of Burl's time these ant-cities rose above the surrounding ground, some small and barely begun, and others ancient colonies which were truly the continuation of cities first built when the ants were insects to be crushed beneath the feet of men. These ancient strongholds towered two, three, and even four hundred feet above the plains, and their inhabitants would have had to be numbered in millions if not billions.

Not all the earth was subject to the ants, however. Bees and wasps and more deadly creatures crawled over and flew above its surface. The bees were four feet and more in length. And slender-waisted wasps darted here and there, preying upon the colossal crickets that sang deep bass music to their mates—and the length of the crickets was the length of a man, and more.

Spiders with bloated bellies waited, motionless, in their snares, whose threads were the size of small cables, waiting for some luckless giant insect to be entangled in the gummy traps. And butterflies fluttered over the festering plains of this new world, tremendous creatures whose wings could only be measured in terms of yards.

An outcropping of rock jutted up abruptly from a fungus-covered plain. Shelf-fungi and strangely colored molds stained the stone until the shining quartz was hidden almost completely from view, but the whole glistened like tinted crystal from the dank wetness of the night. Little wisps of vapor curled away from the slopes as the moisture was taken up by the already moisture-laden air.

Seen from a distance, the outcropping of rock looked innocent and still, but a nearer view showed many things.

Here a hunting wasp had come upon a gray worm, and was methodically inserting its sting into each of the twelve segments of the faintly writhing creature. Presently the worm would be completely paralyzed, and would be carried to the burrow of the wasp, where an egg would be laid upon it, from which a tiny maggot would presently hatch. Then weeks of agony for the great gray worm, conscious, but unable to move, while the maggot fed upon its living flesh—

There the tiny spider, youngest of hatchlings, barely four inches across, stealthily stalked some other still tinier mite, the little, many-legged larva of the oil-beetle, known as the bee-louse. The almost infinitely small bee-louse was barely two inches long, and could easily hide in the thick fur of a great bumblebee.

This one small creature would never fulfill its destiny, however. The hatchling spider sprang—it was a combat of midgets which was soon over.

PLANET NIGHTMARE

When the spider had grown and was feared as a huge, black-bellied tarantula, it would slay monster crickets with the same ease and the same implacable ferocity.

The outcropping of rock looked still and innocent. There was one point where it overhung, forming a shelf, beneath which the stone fell away in a sheer-drop. Many colored fungus growths covered the rock, making it a riot of tints and shades. But hanging from the rooflike projection of the stone there was a strange, drab-white object. It was in the shape of half a globe, perhaps six feet by six feet at its largest. A number of little semicircular doors were fixed about its sides, like inverted arches, each closed by a blank wall. One of them would open, but only one.

The house was like the half of a pallid orange, fastened to the roof of rock. Thick cables stretched in every direction for yards upon yards, anchoring the habitation firmly, but the most striking of the things about the house—still and quiet and innocent, like all the rest of the rock outcropping—were the ghastly trophies fastened to the outer walls and hanging from long silken chains below.

Here was the hind leg of one of the smaller beetles. There was the wing-case of a flying creature. Here a snail-shell, two feet in diameter, hanging at the end of an inch-thick cable. There a boulder that must have weighed thirty or forty pounds, dangling in similar fashion.

But fastened here and there, haphazard and irregularly, were other more repulsive remnants. The shrunken head-armor of a beetle, the fierce jaws of a cricket—the pitiful shreds of a hundred creatures that had formed forgotten meals for the bloated insect within the home.

Comparatively small as was the nest of the clotho spider, it was decorated as no ogre's castle had ever been adorned—legs sucked dry of their contents, corselets of horny armor forever to be unused by any creature, a wing of this insect, the head of that. And dangling by the longest cord of all, with a silken cable wrapped carefully about it to keep the parts together, was the shrunken, shriveled, dried-up body of a long-dead man!

Outside, the nest was a place of gruesome relics. Within, it was a place of luxury and ease. A cushion of softest down filled all the bulging bottom of the hemisphere. A canopy of similarly luxurious texture interposed itself between the rocky roof and the dark, hideous body of the resting spider.

The eyes of the hairy creature glittered like diamonds, even in the darkness, but the loathsome, attenuated legs were tucked under the round-bellied body, and the spider was at rest. It had fed.

It waited, motionless, without desires or aversions, without emotions or perplexities, in comfortable, placid, machinelike contentment until time should bring the call to feed again.

A fresh carcass had been added to the decorations of the nest only the night before. For many days the spider would repose in motionless splendor within the silken castle. When hunger came again, a nocturnal foray, a creature would be pounced upon and slain, brought bodily to the nest, and feasted upon, its body festooned upon the exterior, and another half-sleeping, half-waking period of dreamful idleness within the sybaritic charnel-house would ensue.

Slowly and timidly, half a dozen pink-skinned creatures made their way through the mushroom forest that led to the outcropping of rock under which the clotho spider's nest was slung. They were men, degraded remnants of the once dominant race.

Burl was their leader, and was distinguished solely by two three-foot stumps of the feathery, golden antennæ of a night-flying moth he had bound to his forehead. In his hand was a horny, chitinous spear, taken from the body of an unknown flying creature killed by the flames of the burning purple hills.

Since Burl's return from his solitary—and involuntary—journey, he had been greatly revered by his tribe. Hitherto it had been but a leaderless, formless group of people, creeping to the same hiding-place at nightfall to share in the food of the fortunate, and shudder at the fate of those who might not appear.

Now Burl had walked boldly to them, bearing, upon his back the gray bulk of a labyrinth spider he had slain with his own hands, and clad in wonderful garments of a gorgeousness they envied and admired. They hung upon his words as he struggled to tell them of his adventures, and slowly and dimly they began to look to him for leadership. He was wonderful. For days they had listened breathlessly to the tale of his adventures, but when he demanded that they follow him in another and more perilous affair, they were appalled.

PLANET NIGHTMARE

A peculiar strength of will had come to Burl. He had seen and done things that no man in the memory of his tribe had seen or done. He had stood by when the purple hills burned and formed a funeral pyre for the horde of army ants, and for uncounted thousands of flying creatures. He had caught a leaping tarantula upon the point of his spear, and had escaped from the web of a banded web-spider by oiling his body so that the sticky threads of the snare refused to hold him fast. He had attacked and killed a great gray labyrinth spider.

But most potent of all, he had returned and had been welcomed by Saya—Saya of the swift feet and slender limbs, whose smile roused strange emotions in Burl's breast.

It was the adoring gaze of Saya that had roused Burl to this last pitch of rashness. Months before the clotho spider in the hemispherical silk castle of the gruesome decorations had killed and eaten one of the men of the tribe. Burl and the spider's victim had been together when the spider appeared, and the first faint gray light of morning barely silhouetted the shaggy, horrible creature as it leaped from ambush behind a toadstool toward the fear-stricken pair.

Its attenuated legs were outstretched, its mandibles gaped wide, and its jaws clashed horribly as it formed a black blotch in mid air against the lightening sky.

Burl had fled, screaming, when the other man was seized. Now, however, he was leading half a dozen trembling men toward the inverted dome in which the spider dozed. Two or three of them bore spears like Burl himself, but they bore them awkwardly and timorously. Burl himself was possessed by a strange, fictitious courage. It was the utter recklessness of youth, coupled with the eternal masculine desire to display prowess before a desired female.

The wavering advance came to a halt. Most of the naked men stopped from fear, but Burl stopped to invoke his newly discovered inner self, that had furnished him with such marvelous plans. Quite accidentally he had found that if he persistently asked himself a question, some sort of answer came from within.

Now he gazed up from a safe distance and asked himself how he and the others were to slay the clotho spider. The nest was some forty feet from the ground, on the undersurface of a shelf of rock. There was sheer open space

64

beneath it, but it was firmly held to its support by long, silken cables that curled to the upper side of the rock-shelf, clinging to the stone.

Burl gazed, and presently an idea came to him. He beckoned to the others to follow him, and they did so, their knees knocking together from their fright. At the slightest alarm they would flee, screaming in fear, but Burl did not plan that there should be any alarm.

He led them to the rear of the singular rock formation, up the gently sloping side, and toward the precipitous edge. He drew near the point where the rock fell away. A long, tentacle-like silk cable curled up over the edge of a little promontory of stone that jutted out into nothingness.

Burl began to feel oddly cold, and something of the panic of the other men communicated itself to him. This was one of the anchoring cables that held the spider's castle secure. He looked and found others, six or seven in all, which performed the task of keeping the shaggy, horrid ogre's home from falling to the ground below.

His idea did not desert him, however, and he drew back, to whisper orders to his followers. They obeyed him solely because they were afraid, and he spoke in an authoritative tone, but they did obey, and brought a dozen heavy boulders of perhaps forty pounds weight each.

Burl grasped one of the silken cables at its end and tore it loose from the rock for a space of perhaps two yards. His flesh crawled as he did so, but something within him drove him on. Then, while beads of perspiration stood out on his forehead—induced by nothing less than cold, physical fear—he tied the boulder to the cable. The first one done, he felt emboldened, and made a second fast, and a third.

One of his men stood near the edge of the rock, listening in agonized apprehension. Burl had soon tied a heavy stone to each of the cables he saw, and as a matter of fact, there was but one of them he failed to notice. That one had been covered by the flaking mold that took the place of grass upon the rocky eminence.

There were left upon the promontory, several of the boulders for which there was no use, but Burl did not attempt to double the weights on the cables. He took his followers aside and explained his plan in whispers. Quaking, they agreed, and, trembling, they prepared to carry it out.

One of them stationed himself beside each of the boulders, Burl at the largest. He gave a signal, and half a dozen ripping, tearing sounds broke the sullen silence of the day. The boulders clashed and clattered down the rocky side of the precipice, tearing—perhaps "peeling"—the cables from their adhesion to the stone. They shot into open space and jerked violently at the half-globular nest, which was wrenched from its place by the combined impetus of the six heavy weights.

Burl had flung himself upon his face to watch what he was sure would be the death of the spider as it fell forty feet and more, imprisoned in its heavily weighted home. His eyes sparkled with triumph as he saw the ghastly, trophy-laden house swing out from the cliff. Then he gasped in terror.

One of the cables had not been discovered. That single cable held the spider's castle from a fall, though the nest had been torn from its anchorage, and now dangled heavily on its side in mid air. A convulsive struggle seemed to be going on within.

Then one of the archlike doors opened, and the spider emerged, evidently in terror, and confused by the light of day, but still venomous and still deadly. It found but a single of its anchoring cables intact, that leading to the cliff top hard by Burl's head.

The spider sprang for this single cable, and its legs grasped the slender thread eagerly while it began to climb rapidly up toward the cliff top.

As with all the creatures of Burl's time, its first thought was of battle, not flight, and it came up the thin cord with its poison fangs unsheathed and its mandibles clashing in rage. The shaggy hair upon its body seemed to bristle with insane ferocity, and the horrible, thin legs moved with desperate haste as it hastened to meet and wreak vengeance upon the cause of its sudden alarm.

Burl's followers fled, uttering shrieks of fear, and Burl started to his feet, in the grip of a terrible panic. Then his hand struck one of the heavy boulders. Exerting every ounce of his strength, he pushed it over the cliff just where the cable appeared above the edge. For the fraction of a second there was silence, and then the indescribable sound of an impact against a soft body.

There was a gasping cry, and a moment later the curiously muffled clatter of the boulder striking the earth below. Somehow, the sound suggested that the boulder had struck first upon some soft object.

MURRAY LEINSTER

A faint cry came from the bottom of the hill. The last of Burl's men was leaping to a hiding-place among the mushrooms of the forest, and had seen the sheen of shining armor just before him. He cried out and waited for death, but only a delicately formed wasp rose heavily into the air, bearing beneath it the more and more feebly struggling body of a giant cricket.

Burl had stood paralyzed, deprived of the power of movement, after casting the boulder over the cliff. That one action had taken the last ounce of his initiative, and if the spider had hauled itself over the rocky edge and darted toward him, slavering its thick spittle and uttering sounds of mad fury, Burl would not even have screamed as it seized him. He was like a dead thing. But the oddly muffled sound of the boulder striking the ground below brought back hope of life and power of movement.

He peered over the cliff. The nest still dangled at the end of the single cable, still freighted with its gruesome trophies, but on the ground below a crushed and horribly writhing form was moving in convulsions of rage and agony.

Long, hairy legs worked desperately from a body that was no more than a mass of pulped flesh. A ferocious jaw tried to clamp upon something—and there was no other jaw to meet it. An evil-smelling, sticky liquid exuded from the mangled writhing, thing upon the earth, moving in terrible contortions of torment.

Presently an ant drew near and extended inquisitive antennæ at the helpless monster wounded to death. A shrill stridulation sounded out, and three or four other foot-long ants hastened up to wait patiently just outside the spider's reach until its struggles should have lessened enough to make possible the salvage of flesh from the perhaps still-living creature for the ant city a mile away.

And Burl, up on the cliff-top, danced and gesticulated in triumph. He had killed the clotho spider, which had slain one of the tribesmen four months before. Glory was his. All the tribesmen had seen the spider living. Now he would show them the spider dead. He stopped his dance of triumph and walked down the hill in haughty grandeur. He would reproach his timid followers for fleeing from the spider, leaving him to kill it alone.

Quite naïvely Burl assumed that it was his place to give orders and that of the others to obey. True, no one had attempted to give orders before, or to enforce their execution, but Burl had reached the eminently wholesome conclusion that he was a wonderful person whose wishes should be respected.

Burl, filled with fresh notions of his own importance, strutted on toward the hiding-place of the tribe, growing more and more angry with the other men for having deserted him. He would reproach them, would probably beat them. They would be afraid to protest, and in the future would undoubtedly be afraid to run away.

Burl was quite convinced that running away was something he could not tolerate in his followers. Obscurely—and conveniently in the extreme back of his mind—he reasoned that not only did a larger number of men present at a scene of peril increase the chances of coping with the danger, but they also increased the chances that the victim selected by the dangerous creature would be another than himself.

Burl's reasoning was unsophisticated, but sound; perhaps unconscious, but none the less effective. He grew quite furious with the deserters. They had run away! They had fled from a mere spider.

A shrill whine filled the air, and a ten-inch ant dashed at Burl with its mandibles extended threateningly. Burl's path had promised to interrupt the salvaging work of the insect, engaged in scraping shreds of flesh from the corselet of one of the smaller beetles slain the previous night. The ant dashed at Burl like an infuriated fox-terrier, and Burl scurried away in undignified retreat. The ant might not be dangerous, but bites from its formic acid-poisoned mandibles were no trifles.

Burl came to the tangled thicket of mushrooms in which his tribefolk hid. The entrance was tortuous and difficult to penetrate, and could be blocked on occasion with stones and toadstool pulp. Burl made his way toward the central clearing, and heard as he went the sound of weeping, and the excited chatter of the tribes people.

Those who had fled from the rocky cliff had returned with the news that Burl was dead, and Saya lay weeping beneath an over-shadowing toadstool. She was not yet the mate of Burl, but the time would come when all the tribe would recognize a status dimly different from the usual tribal relationship.

Burl stepped into the clearing, and straightway cuffed the first man he came upon, then the next and the next. There was a cry of astonishment, and the next second instinctive, fearful glances at that entrance to the hiding-place.

Had Burl fled from the spider, and was it following? Burl spoke loftily, saying that the spider was dead, that its legs, each one the length of a man, were still, and its fierce jaws and deadly poison-fangs harmless forevermore.

Ten minutes later he was leading an incredulous, awed little group of pink-skinned people to the spot below the cliff where the spider actually lay dead, with the ants busily at work upon its remains.

And when he went back to the hiding-place he donned again his great cloak that was made from the wing of a magnificent moth, slain by the flames of the purple hills, and sat down in splendor upon a crumbling toadstool, to feast upon the glances of admiration and awe that were sent toward him. Only Saya held back shyly, until he motioned for her to draw near, when she seated herself at his feet and gazed up at him with unutterable adoration in her eyes.

But while Burl basked in the radiance of his tribe's admiration, danger was drawing near them all. For many months there had been strange red mushrooms growing slowly here and there all over the earth, they knew. The tribefolk had speculated about them, but forebore tasting them because they were strange, and strange things were usually dangerous and often fatal.

Now those red growths had ripened and grown ready to emit their spores. Their rounded tops had grown fat, and the tough skin grew taut as if a strange pressure were being applied from within. And to-day, while Burl luxuriated in his position of feared and admired great man of his tribe, at a spot a long distance away, upon a hill-top, one of the red mushrooms burst. The spores inside the taut, tough skin shot all about as if scattered by an explosion, and made a little cloud of reddish, impalpable dust, which hung in the air and moved slowly with the sluggish breeze.

A bee droned into the thin red cloud of dust, lazily and heavily flying back toward the hive. But barely had she entered the tinted atmosphere when her movements became awkward and convulsive, effortful and excited. She trembled and twisted in mid air in a peculiar fashion, then dropped to the earth, while her abdomen moved violently.

Bees, like almost all insects, breathe through spiracles on the undersurfaces of their abdomens. This bee had breathed in some of the red mushroom's spores. She thrashed about desperately upon the toadstools on which she had fallen, struggling for breath, for life.

After a long time she was still. The cloud of red mushroom spores had strangled or poisoned her. And everywhere the red fringe grew, such explosions were taking place, one by one, and wherever the red clouds hung in the air creatures were breathing them in and dying in convulsions of strangulation.

THE JOURNEY

Darkness. The soft, blanketing night of the age of fungoids had fallen over all the earth, and there was blackness everywhere that was not good to have. Here and there, however, dim, bluish lights glowed near the ground. There an intermittent glow showed that a firefly had wandered far from the rivers and swamps above which most of his kind now congregated. Now a faintly luminous ball of fire drifted above the steaming, moisture-sodden earth. It was a will-o'-the-wisp, grown to a yard in diameter.

From the low-hanging banks of clouds that hung perpetually overhead, large, warm raindrops fell ceaselessly. A drop, a pause, and then another drop, added to the already dank moisture of the ground below.

The world of fungus growths flourished on just such dampness and humidity. It seemed as if the toadstools and mushrooms could be heard, swelling and growing large in the darkness. Rustlings and stealthy movements sounded furtively through the night, and from above the heavy throb of mighty wing-beats was continuous.

The tribe was hidden in the midst of a tangled copse of toadstools too thickly interwoven for the larger insects to penetrate. Only the little midgets hid in its recesses during the night-time, and the smaller moths during the day.

About and among the bases of the toadstools, however, where their spongy stalks rose from the humid earth, small beetles roamed, singing cheerfully to themselves in deep bass notes. They were small and round, some six or eight inches long, and their bellies were pale gray.

And as they went about they emitted sounds which would have been chirps had they been other than low as the lowest tone of a harp. They were truffle-beetles, in search of the dainty tidbits on which epicures once had feasted.

MURRAY LEINSTER

Some strange sense seemed to tell them when one of half a dozen varieties of truffle was beneath them, and they paused in their wandering to dig a tunnel straight down. A foot, two feet, or two yards, all was the same to them. In time they would come upon the morsel they sought and would remain at the bottom of their temporary home until it was consumed. Then another period of wandering, singing their cheerful song, until another likely spot was reached and another tunnel begun.

In a tiny, open space in the center of the toadstool thicket the tribefolk slept with the deep notes of the truffle-beetles in their ears. A new danger had come to them, but they had passed it on to Burl with a new and childlike confidence and considered the matter settled. They slept, while beneath a glowing mushroom at one side of the clearing Burl struggled with his new problem. He squatted upon the ground in the dim radiance of the shining toadstool, his moth-wing cloak wrapped about him, his spear in his hand, and his twin golden plumes of the moth's antennæ bound to his forehead. But his face was downcast as a child's.

The red mushrooms had begun to burst. Only that day, one of the women, seeking edible fungus for the tribal larder, had seen the fat, distended globule of the red mushroom. Its skin was stretched taut, and glistened in the light.

The woman paid little or no attention to the red growth. Her ears were attuned to catch sounds that would warn her of danger while her eyes searched for tidbits that would make a meal for the tribe, and more particularly for her small son, left behind at the hiding-place.

A ripping noise made her start up, alert on the instant. The red envelope of the mushroom had split across the top, and a thick cloud of brownish-red dust was spurting in every direction. It formed a pyramidal cloud some thirty feet in height, which enlarged and grew thinner with minor eddies within itself.

A little yellow butterfly with wings barely a yard from tip to tip, flapped lazily above the mushroom-covered plain. Its wings beat the air with strokes that seemed like playful taps upon a friendly element. The butterfly was literally intoxicated with the sheer joy of living. It had emerged from its cocoon barely two hours before, and was making its maiden flight above the strange and wonderful world. It fluttered carelessly into the red-brown cloud of mushroom spores.

71

PLANET NIGHTMARE

The woman was watching the slowly changing form of the spore-mist. She saw the butterfly enter the brownish dust, and then her eyes became greedy. There was something the matter with the butterfly. Its wings no longer moved lazily and gently. They struck out in frenzied, hysterical blows that were erratic and wild. The little yellow creature no longer floated lightly and easily, but dashed here and there, wildly and without purpose, seeming to be in its death-throes.

It crashed helplessly against the ground and lay there, moving feebly. The woman hurried forward. The wings would be new fabric with which to adorn herself, and the fragile legs of the butterfly contained choice meat. She entered the dust-cloud.

A stream of intolerable fire—though the woman had never seen or known of fire—burned her nostrils and seared her lungs. She gasped in pain, and the agony was redoubled. Her eyes smarted as if burning from their sockets, and tears blinded her.

The woman instinctively turned about to flee, but before she had gone a dozen yards—blinded as she was—she stumbled and fell to the ground. She lay there, gasping, and uttering moans of pain, until one of the men of the tribe who had been engaged in foraging near by saw her and tried to find what had injured her.

She could not speak, and he was about to leave her and tell the other tribefolk about her when he heard the clicking of an ant's limbs, and rather than have the ant pick her to pieces bit by bit—and leave his curiosity ungratified—the man put her across his shoulders and bore her back to the hiding-place of the tribe.

It was the tale the woman had told when she partly recovered that caused Burl to sit alone all that night beneath the shining toadstool in the little clearing, puzzling his just-awakened brain to know what to do.

The year before there had been no red mushrooms. They had appeared only recently, but Burl dimly remembered that one day, a long time before, there had been a strange breeze which blew for three day and nights, and that during the time of its blowing all the tribe had been sick and had wept continually.

Burl had not yet reached the point of mental development when he would associate that breeze with a storm at a distance, or reason that the spores of the red mushrooms had been borne upon the wind to the present resting-places of the deadly fungus growths. Still less could he decide that the breeze had not been deadly only because it was lightly laden with the fatal dust.

He knew simply that unknown red mushrooms had appeared, that they were everywhere about, and that they would burst, and that to breathe the red dust they gave out was grievous sickness or death.

The tribe slept while the bravely attired figure of Burl squatted under the glowing disk of the luminous mushroom, his face a picture of querulous perplexity, and his heart full of sadness.

He had consulted his strange inner self, and no plan had come to him. He knew the red mushrooms were all about. They would fill the air with their poison. He struggled with his problem while his people slumbered, and the woman who had breathed the mushroom-dust sobbed softly in her troubled sleep.

Presently a figure stirred on the farther side of the clearing. Saya woke and raised her head. She saw Burl crouching by the shining toadstool, his gay attire draggled and unnoticed. She watched him for a little, and the desolation of his pose awoke her pity.

She rose and went to his side, taking his hand between her two, while she spoke his name softly. When he turned and looked at her, confusion smote her, but the misery in his face brought confidence again.

Burl's sorrow was inarticulate—he could not explain this new responsibility for his people that had come to him—but he was comforted by her presence, and she sat down beside him. After a long time she slept, with her head resting against his side, but he continued to question himself, continued to demand an escape for his people from the suffering and danger he saw ahead. With the day an answer came.

When Burl had been carried down the river on his fungus raft, and had landed in the country of the army ants, he had seen great forests of edible mushrooms, and had said to himself that he would bring Saya to that place. He remembered, now, that the red mushrooms were there also, but the idea of a journey remained.

The hunting-ground of his tribe had been free of the red fungoids until recently. If he traveled far enough he would come to a place where there were still no red toadstools. Then came the decision. He would lead his tribe to a far country.

PLANET NIGHTMARE

He spoke with stern authority when the tribesmen woke, talking in few words and in a loud voice, holding up his spear as he gave his orders.

The timid, pink-skinned people obeyed him meekly. They had seen the body of the clotho spider he had slain, and he had thrown down before them the gray bulk of the labyrinth spider he had thrust through with his spear. Now he was to take them through unknown dangers to an unknown haven, but they feared to displease him.

They made light loads of their mushrooms and such meat-stuffs as they had, and parceled out what little fabric they still possessed. Three men bore spears, in addition to Burl's long shaft, and he had persuaded the other three to carry clubs, showing them how the weapon should be wielded.

The indefinitely brighter spot in the cloud-banks above that meant the shining sun had barely gone a quarter of the way across the sky when the trembling band of timid creatures made their way from their hiding-place and set out upon their journey. For their course, Burl depended entirely upon chance. He avoided the direction of the river, however, and the path along which he had returned to his people. He knew the red mushrooms grew there. Purely by accident he set his march toward the west, and walked cautiously on, his tribesfolk following him fearfully.

Burl walked ahead, his spear held ready. He made a figure at once brave and pathetic, venturing forth in a world of monstrous ferocity and incredible malignance, armed only with a horny spear borrowed from a dead insect. His velvety cloak, made from a moth's wing, hung about his figure in graceful folds, however, and twin golden plumes nodded jauntily from his forehead.

Behind him the nearly naked people followed reluctantly. Here a woman with a baby in her arms, there children of nine or ten, unable to resist the Instinct to play even in the presence of the manifold dangers of the march. They ate hungrily of the lumps of mushroom they had been ordered to carry. Then a long-legged boy, his eyes roving anxiously about in search of danger followed.

Thirty thousand years of flight from every peril had deeply submerged the combative nature of humanity. After the boy came two men, one with a short spear, and the other with a club, each with a huge mass of edible mushroom under his free arm, and both badly frightened at the idea of

74

fleeing from dangers they knew and feared to dangers they did not know and consequently feared much more.

So was the caravan spread out. It made its way across the country with many deviations from a fixed line, and with many halts and pauses. Once a shrill stridulation filled all the air before them, a monster sound compounded of innumerable clickings and high-pitched cries.

They came to the tip of an eminence and saw a great space of ground covered with tiny black bodies locked in combat. For quite half a mile in either direction the earth was black with ants, snapping and biting at each other, locked in vise-like embraces, each combatant couple trampled under the feet of the contending armies, with no thought of surrender or quarter.

The sound of the clashing of fierce jaws upon horny armor, the cries of the maimed, and strange sounds made by the dying, and above all, the whining battle-cry of each of the fighting hordes, made a sustained uproar that was almost deafening.

From either side of the battle-ground a pathway led back to separate ant-cities, a pathway marked by the hurrying groups of reinforcements rushing to the fight. Tiny as the ants were, for once no lumbering beetle swaggered insolently in their path, nor did the hunting-spiders mark them out for prey. Only little creatures smaller than the combatants themselves made use of the insect war for purposes of their own.

These were little gray ants barely more than four inches long, who scurried about in and among the fighting creatures with marvelous dexterity, carrying off, piece-meal, the bodies of the dead, and slaying the wounded for the same fate.

They hung about the edges of the battle, and invaded the abandoned areas when the tide of battle shifted, insect guerrillas, fighting for their own hands, careless of the origin of the quarrel, espousing no cause, simply salvaging the dead and living débris of the combat.

Burl and his little group of followers had to make a wide detour to avoid the battle itself, and the passage between bodies of reinforcements hurrying to the scene of strife was a matter of some difficulty. The ants running rapidly toward the battle-field were hugely excited. Their antennæ waved wildly, and the infrequent wounded one, limping back toward the city, was instantly and repeatedly challenged by the advancing insects.

They crossed their antennæ upon his, and required thorough evidence that he was of the proper city before allowing him to proceed. Once they arrived at the battle-field they flung themselves into the fray, becoming lost and indistinguishable in the tide of straining, fighting black bodies.

Men in such a battle, without distinguishing marks or battle-cries, would have fought among themselves as often as against their foes, but the ants had a much simpler method of identification. Each ant-city possesses its individual odor—a variant on the scent of formic acid—and each individual of that city is recognized in his world quite simply and surely by the way he smells.

The little tribe of human beings passed precariously behind a group of a hundred excited insect warriors, and before the following group of forty equally excited black insects. Burl hurried on with his following, putting many miles of perilous territory behind before nightfall. Many times during the day they saw the sudden billowing of a red-brown dust-cloud from the earth, and more than once they came upon the empty skin and drooping stalk of one of the red mushrooms, and more often still they came upon the mushrooms themselves, grown fat and taut, prepared to send their deadly spores into the air when the pressure from within became more than the leathery skin could stand.

That night the tribe hid among the bases of giant puff-balls, which at a touch shot out a puff of white powder resembling smoke. The powder was precisely the same in nature as that cast out by the red mushrooms, but its effects were marvelously—and mercifully—different; it was innocuous.

Burl slept soundly this night, having been two days and a night without rest, but the remainder of his tribe, and even Saya, were fearful and afraid, listening ceaselessly all through the dark hours for the menacing sounds of creatures coming to prey upon them.

And so for a week the march kept on. Burl would not allow his tribe to stop to forage for food. The red mushrooms were all about. Once one of the little children was caught in a whirling eddy of red dust, and its mother rushed into the deadly stuff to seize it and bring it out. Then the tribe had to hide for three days while the two of them recovered from the debilitating poison.

Once, too, they found a half-acre patch of the giant cabbages—there were six of them full grown, and a dozen or more smaller ones—and Burl took two men and speared two of the huge, twelve-foot slugs that fed upon the leaves. When the tribe passed on it was gorged on the fat meat of the slugs, and there was much soft fur, so that all the tribefolk wore loin-cloths of the yellow stuff.

There were perils, too, in the journey. On the fourth day of the tribe's traveling, Burl froze suddenly into stillness. One of the hairy tarantulas—a trap-door spider with a black belly—had fallen upon a scarabæus beetle, and was devouring it only a hundred yards ahead.

The tribefolk, trembling, went back for half a mile or more in panic-stricken silence, and refused to advance until he had led them a detour of two or three miles to one side of the dangerous spot.

Long, fear-ridden marches through perilous countries unknown to them, through the golden aisles of yellow mushroom forests, over the flaking surfaces of plains covered with many-colored "rusts" and molds; pauses beside turbid pools whose waters were concealed by thick layers of green slime, and other evil-smelling ponds which foamed and bubbled slowly, which were covered with pasty yeasts that rose in strange forms of discolored foam.

Fleeting glimpses they had of the glistening spokes of symmetrical spiders'-webs, whose least thread it would have been beyond the power of the strongest of the tribe to break. They passed through a forest of puff-balls, which boomed when touched and shot a puff of vapor from their open mouths.

Once they saw a long and sinuous insect that fled before them and disappeared into a burrow in the ground, running with incredible speed upon legs of uncountable number. It was a centipede all of thirty feet in length, and when they crossed the path it had followed a horrible stench came to their nostrils so that they hurried on.

Long escape from unguessed dangers brought boldness, of a sort, to the pink-skinned men, and they would have rested. They went to Burl with their complaint, and he simply pointed with his hands behind them. There were three little clouds of brownish vapor in the air, where they could see, along the road they had traversed. To the right of them a dust-cloud was just settling, and to the left another rose as they looked.

A new trick of the deadly dust became apparent now. Toward the end of a day in which they had traveled a long distance, one of the little children ran a little to the left of the route its elders were following. The earth had taken on a brownish hue, and the child stirred up the surface mould with its feet.

The brownish dust that had settled there was raised again, and the child ran, crying and choking, to its mother, its lungs burning as with fire, and its eyes like hot coals. Another day would pass before the child could walk.

In a strange country, knowing nothing of the dangers that might assail the tribe while waiting for the child to recover, Burl looked about for a hiding-place. Far over to the right a low cliff, perhaps twenty or thirty feet high, showed sides of crumbling, yellow clay, and from where Burl stood he could see the dark openings of burrows scattered here and there upon its face.

He watched for a time, to see if any bee or wasp inhabited them, knowing that many kinds of both insects dig burrows for their young, and do not occupy them themselves. No dark forms appeared, however, and he led his people toward the openings.

The appearance of the holes confirmed his surmise. They had been dug months before by mining bees, and the entrances were "weathered" and worn. The tribefolk made their way into the three-foot tunnels, and hid themselves, seizing the opportunity to gorge themselves upon the food they carried.

Burl stationed himself near the outer end of one of the little caves to watch for signs of danger. While waiting he poked curiously with his spear at a little pile of white and sticky parchment-like stuff he saw just within the mouth of the tunnel.

Instantly movement became visible. Fifty, sixty, or a hundred tiny creatures, no more than half an inch in length, tumbled pell-mell from the dirty-white heap. Awkward legs, tiny, greenish-black bodies, and bristles protruding in every direction made them strange to look upon.

They had tumbled from the whitish heap and now they made haste to hide themselves in it again, moving slowly and clumsily, with immense effort and laborious contortions of their bodies.

Burl had never seen any insect progress in such a slow and ineffective fashion before. He drew one little insect back with the point of his spear and examined it from a safe distance. Tiny jaws before the head met like twin sickles, and the whole body was shaped like a rounded diamond lozenge.

Burl knew that no insect of such small size could be dangerous, and leaned over, then took one creature in his hand. It wriggled frantically and slipped from his fingers, dropping upon the soft yellow caterpillar-fur he had about his middle. Instantly, as if it were a conjuring trick, the little insect vanished, and Burl searched for a matter of minutes before he found it hidden deep in the long, soft hairs of the fur, resting motionless, and evidently at ease.

It was a bee-louse, the first larval form of a beetle whose horny armor could be seen in fragments for yards before the clayey cliff-side. Hidden in the openings of the bee's tunnel, it waited until the bee-grubs farther back in their separate cells should complete their changes of form and emerge into the open air, passing over the cluster of tiny creatures at the doorway. As the bees pass, the little bee-lice would clamber in eager haste up their hairy legs and come to rest in the fur about their thoraxes. Then, weeks later, when the bees in turn made other cells and stocked them with honey for the eggs they would lay, the tiny creatures would slip from their resting-places and be left behind in the fully provisioned cell, to eat not only the honey the bee had so laboriously acquired, but the very grub hatched from the bee's egg.

Burl had no difficulty in detaching the small insect and casting it away, but in doing so discovered three more that had hidden themselves in his furry garment, no doubt thinking it the coat of their natural, though unwilling hosts. He plucked them away, and discovered more, and more. His garment was the hiding-place for dozens of the creatures.

Disgusted and annoyed, he went out of the cavern and to a spot some distance away, where he took off his robe and pounded it with the flat side of his spear to dislodge the visitors. They dropped out one by one, reluctantly, and finally the garment was clean of them. Then Burl heard a shout from the direction of the mining-bee caves, and hastened toward the sound.

It was then drawing toward the time of darkness, but one of the tribesmen had ventured out and found no less than three of the great imperial mushrooms. Of the three, one had been attacked by a parasitic purple mould, but the gorgeous yellow of the other two was undimmed, and the people were soon feasting upon the firm flesh.

Burl felt a little pang of jealousy, though he joined in the consumption of the find as readily as the others, and presently drew a little to one side.

He cast his eyes across the country, level and unbroken as far as the eye could see. The small clay cliff was the only inequality visible, and its height cut off all vision on one side. But the view toward the horizon was unobstructed on three sides, and here and there the black speck of a monster bee could be seen, droning homeward to its hive or burrow, and sometimes the slender form of a wasp passed overhead, its transparent wings invisible from the rapidity of their vibrations.

These flew high in the air, but lower down, barely skimming the tops of the many-colored mushrooms and toadstools, fluttering lightly above the swollen fungoids, and touching their dainty proboscides to unspeakable things in default of the fragrant flowers that were normal food for their races—lower down flew the multitudes of butterflies the age of mushrooms had produced.

White and yellow and red and brown, pink and blue and purple and green, every shade and every color, every size and almost every shape, they flitted gaily in the air. There were some so tiny that they would barely have shaded Burl's face, and some beneath whose slender bodies he could have hidden himself. They flew in a riot of colors and tints above a world of foul mushroom growths, and turgid, slime-covered ponds.

Burl, temporarily out of the limelight because of the discovery of a store of food by another member of the tribe, bethought himself of an idea. Soon night would come on, the cloud-bank would turn red in the west, and then darkness would lean downward from the sky. With the coming of that time these creatures of the day would seek hiding-places, and the air would be given over to the furry moths that flew by night. He, Burl, would mark the spot where one of the larger creatures alighted, and would creep up upon it, with his spear held fast.

His wide blue eyes brightened at the thought, and he sat himself down to watch. After a long time the soft, down-reaching fingers of the night touched the shaded aisles of the mushroom forests, and a gentle haze arose above the golden glades. One by one the gorgeous fliers of the daytime dipped down and furled their painted wings. The overhanging clouds became darker—finally black, and the slow, deliberate rainfall that lasted all through the night began. Burl rose and crept away into the darkness, his spear held in readiness.

Through the black night, beneath deeper blacknesses which were the dark undersides of huge toadstools, creeping silently, with every sense alert for sign of danger or for hope of giant prey, Burl made his slow advance.

A glorious butterfly of purple and yellow markings, whose wings spread out for three yards on either side of its delicately formed body, had hidden itself barely two hundred yards away. Burl could imagine it, now, preening its slender limbs and combing from its long and slender proboscis any trace of the delectable foodstuffs on which it had fed during the day. Burl moved slowly and cautiously forward, all eyes and ears.

He heard an indescribable sound in a thicket a little to his left, and shifted his course. The sound was the faint whistling of air through the breathing-holes along an insect's abdomen. Then came the delicate rustling of filmy wings being stretched and closed again, and the movement of sharply barbed feet upon the soft earth. Burl moved in breathless silence, holding his spear before him in readiness to plunge it into the gigantic butterfly's soft body.

The mushrooms here were grown thickly together, so there was no room for Burl's body to pass between their stalks, and the rounded heads were deformed and misshapen from their crowdings. Burl spent precious moments in trying to force a silent passage, but had to own himself beaten. Then he clambered up upon the spongy mass of mushroom heads, trusting to luck that they would sustain his weight.

The blackness was intense, so that even the forms of objects before him were lost in obscurity. He moved forward for some ten yards, however, walking gingerly over his precarious foothold. Then he felt rather than saw the opening before him. A body moved below him.

Burl raised his spear, and with a yell plunged down on the back of the moving thing, thrusting his spear with all the force he could command. He landed on a shifting form, but his yell of triumph turned to a scream of terror.

This was not the yielding body of a slender butterfly that he had come upon, nor had his spear penetrated the creature's soft flesh. He had fallen upon the shining back of one of the huge, meat-eating beetles, and his spear had slid across the horny armor, and then stuck fast, having pierced only the leathery tissue between the insect's head and thorax.

Burl's terror was pitiable at the realization, but as nothing to the ultimate panic which possessed him when the creature beneath him uttered a grunt of fright and pain, and, spreading its stiff wing-cases wide, shot upward in a crazy, panic-stricken, rocket-like flight toward the sky.

THE SEXTON-BEETLES

Burl fell headforemost upon the spongy top of a huge toadstool that split with the impact and let him through to the ground beneath, powdering him with its fine spores. He came to rest with his naked shoulder half-way through the yielding flesh of a mushroom-stalk, and lay there for a second, catching his breath to scream again.

Then he heard the whining buzz of his attempted prey. There was something wrong with the beetle. Burl's spear had struck it in an awkward spot, and it was rocketing upward in erratic flight that ended in a crash two or three hundreds yards away.

Burl sprang up in an instant. Perhaps, despite his mistake, he had slain this infinitely more worthy victim. He rushed toward the spot where it had fallen.

His wide blue eyes pierced the darkness well enough to enable him to sheer off from masses of toadstools, but he could distinguish no details—nothing but forms. He heard the beetle floundering upon the ground; then heard it mount again into the air, more clumsily than before.

Its wing-beats no longer kept up a sustained note. They thrashed the air irregularly and wildly. The flight was zigzag and uncertain, and though longer than the first had been, it ended similarly, in a heavy fall. Another period of floundering, and the beetle took to the air again just before Burl arrived at the spot.

It was obviously seriously hurt, and Burl forgot the dangers of the night in his absorption in the chase. He darted after his prey, fleet-footed and agile, taking chances that in cold blood he would never have thought of.

Twice, in the pain-racked struggles of the monster beetle, he arrived at the spot where the gigantic insect flung itself about madly, insanely, fighting it knew not what, striking out with colossal wings and legs, dazed and drunk with agony. And each time it managed to get aloft in flight that was weaker and more purposeless.

Crazy, fleeing from the torturing spear that pierced its very vitals, the beetle blundered here and there, floundering among the mushroom thickets in spasms that were constantly more prolonged and more agonized, but nevertheless flying heavily, lurching drunkenly, managing to graze the tops of the toadstools in one more despairing, tormented flight.

And Burl followed, aflame with the fire of the chase, arriving at the scene of each successive, panic-stricken struggle on the ground just after the beetle had taken flight again, but constantly more closely on the heels of the weakening monster.

At last he came up panting, and found the giant lying upon the earth, moving feebly, apparently unable to rise. How far he was from the tribe, Burl did not know, nor did the question occur to him at the moment. He waited for the beetle to be still, trembling with excitement and eagerness. The struggles of the huge form grew more feeble, and at last ceased. Burl moved forward and grasped his spear. He wrenched at it to thrust again.

In an instant the beetle had roused itself, and was exerting its last atom of strength, galvanized into action by the agony caused by Burl's seizure of the spear. A great wing-cover knocked Burl twenty feet, and flung him against the base of a mushroom, where he lay, half stunned. But then a strangely pungent scent came to his nostrils—the scent of the red mushrooms!

He staggered to his feet and fled, while behind him the gigantic beetle crashed and floundered—Burl heard a tearing and ripping sound. The insect had torn the covering of one of the red mushrooms, tightly packed with the fatal red dust. At the noise, Burl's speed was doubled, but he could still hear the frantic struggles of the dying beetle grow to a very crescendo of desperation.

The creature broke free and managed to rise in a final flight, fighting for breath and life, weakened and tortured by the spear and the horrible spores of the red mushrooms. Then it crashed suddenly to the earth and was still. The red dust had killed it.

In time to come, Burl might learn to use the red dust as poison gas had been used by his ancestors of thirty thousand years before, but now he was frightened and alone, lost from his tribe, and with no faintest notion of how to find them. He crouched beneath a huge toadstool and waited for dawn, listening with terrified apprehension for the ripping sound that would mean the bursting of another of the red mushrooms.

Only the wing beats of night-flying creatures came to his ears, however, and the discordant noises of the four-foot truffle-beetles as they roamed the aisles of the mushroom forests, seeking the places beneath which their instinct told them fungoid dainties awaited the courageous miner. The eternal dripping of the raindrops falling at long intervals from the overhanging clouds formed a soft obbligato to the whole.

Burl listened, knowing there were red toadstools all about, but not once during the whole of the long, dark hours did the rending noise tell of a bursting fungus casting loose its freight of deadly dust upon the air. Only when day came again, and the chill dampness of the night was succeeded by the steaming humidity of the morning, did a tall pyramid of brownish-red stuff leap suddenly into the air from a ripped mushroom covering.

Then Burl stood up and looked around. Here and there, all over the whole countryside, slowly and at intervals, the cones of fatal red sprang into the air. Had Burl lived thirty thousand years earlier, he might have likened the effect to that of shells bursting from a leisurely bombardment, but as it was he saw in them only fresh and inexorable dangers added to an already peril-ridden existence.

A hundred yards from where he had hidden during the night the body of his victim lay, crumpled up and limp. Burl approached speculatively. He had come even before the ants appeared to take their toll of the carcass, and not even a buzzing flesh-fly had placed its maggots on the unresisting form.

The long, whiplike antennæ lay upon the carpet of mold and rust, and the fiercely toothed legs were drawn close against the body. The many-faceted eyes stared unseeingly, and the stiff and horny wing-cases were rent and torn.

When Burl went to the other side of the dead beetle he saw something that filled him with elation. His spear had been held between his body and the beetle's during that mad flight, and at the final crash, when Burl shot away from the fear-crazed insect, the weight of his body had forced the spearpoint between the joints of the corselet and the neck. Even if the red dust had not finished the creature, the spear wound in time would have ended its life.

Burl was thrilled once more by his superlative greatness, and conveniently forgot that it was the red dust that had actually administered the *coup de grâce*. It was so much more pleasant to look upon himself as the mighty slayer that he hacked off one of the barb-edged limbs to carry back to his tribe in evidence of his feat. He took the long antennæ, too, as further proof.

Then he remembered that he did not know where his tribe was to be found. He had no faintest idea of the direction in which the beetle had flown. As a matter of fact, the course of the beetle had been in turn directed toward every point of the compass, and there was no possible way of telling the relation of its final landing-place to the point from which it had started.

Burl wrestled with his problem for an hour, and then gave up in disgust. He set off at random, with the leg of the huge insect flung over his shoulder and the long antennæ clasped in his hand with his spear. He turned to look at his victim of the night before just before plunging into the near-by mushroom forest, and saw that it was already the center of a mass of tiny black bodies, pulling and hacking at the tough armor, and carving out great lumps of the succulent flesh to be carried to the near-by ant city.

In the teeming life of the insect world death is an opportunity for the survivors. There is a strangely tense and fearful competition for the bodies of the slain. There had been barely an hour of daylight in which the ants might seek for provender, yet in that little time the freshly killed beetle had been found and was being skilfully and carefully exploited. When the body of one of the larger insects fell to the ground, there was a mighty rush, a fierce race, among all the tribes of scavengers to see who should be first.

Usually the ants had come upon the scene and were inquisitively exploring the carcass long before even the flesh-flies had arrived, who dropped their living maggots upon the creature. The blue-bottles came still later, to daub their masses of white eggs about the delicate membranes of the eye.

And while all the preceding scavengers were at work, furtive beetles and tiny insects burrowed below the reeking body to attack the highly scented flesh from a fresh angle.

Each working independently of the others, they commonly appeared in the order of the delicacy of the sense which could lead them to a source of food, though accident could and sometimes did afford one group of workers in putrescence an advantage over the others.

Thus, sometimes a blue-bottle anticipated even the eager ants, and again the very flesh-flies dropped their squirming offspring upon a limp form that was already being undermined by white-bellied things working in the darkness below the body.

Burl grimaced at the busy ants and buzzing flies, and disappeared into the mushroom forest. Here for a long time he moved cautiously and silently through the aisles of tangled stalks and the spongy, round heads of the fungoids. Now and then he saw one of the red toadstools, and made a wide detour around it. Twice they burst within his sight, circumscribed as his vision was by the toadstools among which he was traveling.

Each time he ran hastily to put as much distance as possible between himself and the deadly red dust. He traveled for an hour or more, looking constantly for familiar landmarks that might guide him to his tribe. He knew that if he came upon any place he had seen while with his tribe he could follow the path they had traveled and in time rejoin them.

For many hours he went on, alert for signs of danger. He was quite ignorant of the fact that there were such things as points of the compass, and though he had a distinct notion that he was not moving in a straight line, he did not realize that he was actually moving in a colossal half-circle. After walking steadily for nearly four hours he was no more than three miles in a direct line from his starting-point. As it happened, his uncertainty of direction was fortunate.

The night before the tribe had been feeding happily upon one of the immense edible mushrooms, when they heard Burl's abruptly changing cry. It had begun as a shout of triumph, and ended as a scream of fear. Then they heard hurried wing-beats as a creature rose into the air in a scurry of desperation. The throbbing of huge wings ended in a heavy fall, followed by another flight.

Velvety darkness masked the sky, and the tribesmen could only stare off into the blackness, where their leader had vanished, and begin to tremble, wondering what they should do in a strange country with no bold chief to guide them.

He was the first man to whom the tribe had ever offered allegiance, but their submission had been all the more complete for that fact, and his loss was the more appalling.

Burl had mistaken their lack of timidity. He had thought it independence, and indifference to him. As a matter of fact, it was security because the tribe felt safe under his tutelage. Now that he had vanished, and in a fashion that seemed to mean his death, their old fears returned to them reenforced by the strangeness of their surroundings.

They huddled together and whispered their fright to one another, listening the while in panic-stricken apprehension for signs of danger. The tribesmen visualized Burl caught in fiercely toothed limbs, being rent and torn in mid air by horny, insatiable jaws, his blood falling in great spurts toward the earth below. They caught a faint, reedy cry, and shuddered, pressing closer together.

And so through the long night they waited in trembling silence. Had a hunting spider appeared among them they would not have lifted a hand to defend themselves, but would have fled despairingly, would probably have scattered and lost touch with one another, and spent the remainder of their lives as solitary fugitives, snatching fear-ridden rest in strange hiding-places.

But day came again, and they looked into each other's eyes, reading in each the selfsame panic and fear. Saya was probably the most pitiful of all the group. Burl was to have been her mate, and her face was white and drawn beyond that of any of the rest of the tribefolk.

With the day, they did not move, but remained clustered about the huge mushroom on which they had been feeding the night before. They spoke in hushed and fearful tones, huddled together, searching all the horizon for insect enemies. Saya would not eat, but sat still, staring before her in unseeing indifference. Burl was dead.

A hundred yards from where they crouched a red mushroom glistened in the pale light of the new day. Its tough skin was taut and bulging, resisting the pressure of the spores within. But slowly, as the morning wore on, some of the moisture that had kept the skin soft and flaccid during the night evaporated.

The skin had a strong tendency to contract, like green leather when drying. The spores within it strove to expand. The opposing forces produced a tension that grew greater and greater as more and more of the moisture was absorbed by the air. At last the skin could hold no longer.

With a ripping sound that could be heard for hundreds of feet, the tough wrapping split and tore across its top, and with a hollow, booming noise the compressed mass of deadly spores rushed into the air, making a pyramidal cloud of brown-red dust some sixty feet in height.

The tribesmen quivered at the noise and faced the dust cloud for a fleeting instant, then ran pell-mell to escape the slowly moving tide of death as the almost imperceptible breeze wafted it slowly toward them. Men and women, boys and girls, they fled in a mad rush from the deadly stuff, not pausing to see that even as it advanced it settled slowly to the ground, nor stopping to observe its path that they might step aside and let it go safely by.

Saya fled with the rest, but without their extreme panic. She fled because the others had done so, and ran more carelessly, struggling with a half-formed idea that it did not particularly matter whether she were caught or not.

She fell slightly behind the others, without being noticed. Then quite abruptly a stone turned under her foot, and she fell headlong, striking her head violently against a second stone. Then she lay quite still while the red cloud billowed slowly toward her, drifting gently in the faint, hardly perceptible breeze.

It drew nearer and nearer, settling slowly, but still a huge and menacing mass of deadly dust. It gradually flattened out, too, so that though it had been a rounded cone at first, it flowed over the minor inequalities of the ground as a huge and tenuous leech might have crawled, sucking from all breathing creatures the life they had within them.

A hundred and fifty yards away, a hundred yards away, then only fifty yards away. From where Saya lay unconscious on the earth, eddies within the moving mass could be seen, and the edges took on a striated appearance, telling of the curling of the dust wreaths in the larger mass of deadly powder.

The deliberate advance kept on, seeming almost purposeful. It would have seemed possible to draw from the unhurried, menacing movement of the poisonous stuff that some malign intelligence was concealed in it, that it was, in fact, a living creature. But when the misty edges of the cloud were no more than twenty-five yards from Saya's prostrate body a breeze from one side sprang up—a vagrant, fitful little breeze, that first halted the red cloud and threw it into confusion and then drove it to one side, so that it passed Saya without harming her, though a single trailing wisp of dark-red mist floated very close to her.

Then for a time Saya lay still indeed, only her breast rising and falling gently with faint and irregular breaths. Her head had struck a sharp-edged stone in her fall, and a tiny pool of sticky red had gathered from the wound.

Perhaps thirty feet from where she lay, three small toadstools grew in a little clump, their bases so close together that they seemed but one. From between two of them, however, just where they parted, twin tufts of reddish threads appeared, twinkling back and forth, and in and out. As if they had given some reassuring sign, two slender antennæ followed, then bulging eyes, and then a small black body which had bright-red scalloped markings upon the wing-cases.

It was a tiny beetle no more than eight inches long—a burying-beetle. It drew near Saya's body and clambered upon her, explored the ground by her side, moving all the time in feverish haste, and at last dived into the ground beneath her shoulder, casting back a little shower of hastily dug earth as it disappeared.

Ten minutes later another similar insect appeared, and upon the heels of the second a third. Each of them made the same hasty examination, and each dived under the still form. Presently the earth seemed to billow at a spot along Saya's side, then at another. Perhaps ten minutes after the arrival of the third beetle a little rampart had reared itself all about Saya's body, precisely following the outline of her form. Then her body moved slightly, in a number of tiny jerks, and seemed to settle perhaps half an inch into the ground.

The burying beetles were of those who exploited the bodies of the fallen. Working from below, they excavated the earth from the under side of such prizes as they came upon, then turned upon their backs and thrust with their legs, jerking the body so it sank into the shallow excavation they had prepared.

The process would be repeated until at last the whole of the gift of fortune had sunk below the surrounding surface and the loosened earth fell in upon the top, thus completing the inhumation.

Then in the darkness the beetles would feast and rear their young, gorging upon the plentiful supply of succulent foodstuff they had hidden from jealous fellow scavengers above them.

But Saya was alive. Thirty thousand years before, when scientists examined into the habits of the burying-beetles, or the sexton-beetles, they had declared that fresh meat or living meat would not be touched. They based their statement solely upon the fact that the insects (then tiny creatures indeed) did not appear until the trap-meat placed by the investigators had remained untouched for days.

Conditions had changed in thirty thousand years. The ever-present ants and the sharp-eyed flies were keen rivals of the brightly arrayed beetles. Usually the tribes of creatures who worked in the darkness below ground came after the ants had taken their toll, and the flies sipped daintily.

When Saya fell unconscious upon the ground, however, it was the one accident that caused the burying-beetle to find her first, before the ants had come to tear the flesh from her slender, soft-skinned body. She breathed gently and irregularly, her face drawn with the sorrow of the night before, while desperately hurrying beetles swarmed beneath her body, channeling away the earth so that she would sink lower and lower into the ground.

An inch, and a long wait. Then she sank slowly a second inch. The bright-red tufts of thread appeared again, and a beetle made his way to the open air. He moved hastily about, inspecting the progress of the work. He dived below again. Another inch, and after a long time another inch was excavated.

Burl stepped out from a group of over-shadowing toadstools and halted. He cast his eyes over the landscape, and was struck by its familiarity. It was, in point of fact, very near the spot he had left the night before, in pursuit of a colossal wounded beetle.

Burl moved back and forth, trying to account for the sensation of recognition, and then trying to approximate the place from which he had last seen it.

He passed within fifty feet of the spot where Saya lay, now half buried in the ground. The loose earth cast up about her body had begun to fall in little rivulets upon her. One of her shoulders was already screened from view.

Burl passed on, unseeing. He was puzzling over the direction from which he had seen the particular section of countryside before him. Perhaps a little farther on he would come to the place. He hurried a little. In a moment he recognized his location. There was the great edible mushroom, half broken away, from which the tribe had been feeding. There were the mining bee burrows.

His feet stirred up a fine dust, and he stopped short. A red mushroom had covered the earth with a thin layer of its impalpable, deadly powder. Burl understood why the tribe had gone, and a cold sweat came upon his body. Was Saya safe, or had the whole tribe succumbed to the poisonous stuff? Had they all, men and women and children, died in convulsions of gasping strangulation?

He hurried to retrace his footsteps. There was a fragment of mushrooms on the ground. Here was a spear, cast away by one of the tribesmen in his flight. Burl broke into a run.

The little excavation into which Saya was sinking, inch by inch, was all of twenty-five feet to the right of the path. Burl dashed on, frantic with anxiety about the tribe, but most of all about Saya. Saya's body quivered and sank a fraction more into the earth.

Half a dozen little rivulets of dirt were tumbling upon her body now. In a matter of minutes she would be hidden from view. Burl ran madly past her, too busy searching the mushroom thickets before him with his eyes to dream of looking upon the ground.

Twenty yards from a huge toadstool thicket a noise arrested him sharply. There was a crashing and breaking of the brittle, spongy growths. Twin tapering antennæ appeared, and then a monster beetle lurched into the open space, its horrible, gaping jaws stretched wide.

It was all of eight feet long, and its body was held up from the ground by six crooked, saw-toothed limbs. Its huge multiple eyes stared with machinelike preoccupation at the world.

It advanced deliberately, with a clanking and clashing as of a hideous machine. Burl fled on the instant, running as madly away from the beetle as he had a moment before been running toward it.

A little depression in the earth was before him. He did not swerve, but made to leap it. As he shot over it, however, the glint of pink skin caught his eye, and there was impressed upon his brain with photographic completeness the picture of Saya, lying limp and helpless, sinking slowly into the ground, with tiny rills of earth falling down the sides of the excavation upon her. It seemed to Burl's eye that she quivered slightly as he saw.

There was a terrific struggle within Burl. Behind him the colossal meat-eating beetle. Beneath him Saya, whom he loved. There was certain death lurching toward him on evilly glittering legs, and there was life for his race and tribe lying in the shallow pit.

He turned, aware with a sudden reckless glow that he was throwing away his life, aware that he was deliberately giving himself over to death, and stood on the side of the little pit nearest the great beetle, his puny spear held defiantly at the ready. In his left hand he held just such a leg as those which bore the living creature toward him. He had torn it from the body of just such a monster but a few hours ago, a monster in whose death he had had a share. With a yell of insane defiance, he flung the fiercely toothed limb at his advancing opponent.

The sharp teeth cut into the base of one of the beetle's antennæ, and it ducked clumsily, then seized the missile in its fierce jaws and crushed it in frenzy of rage. There was meat within it, sweet and juicy meat that pleased the beetle's palate.

It forgot the man, standing there, waiting for death. It crunched the missile that had attacked it, eating the palatable contents of the horny armor, confusing the blow with the object that had delivered it, and evidently satisfied that an enemy had been conquered and was being devoured. A moment later it turned and lumbered off to investigate another mushroom thicket.

And Burl turned quickly and dragged Saya's limp form from the grave that had been prepared for it by the busy insect scavengers. Earth fell from her shoulders, from her hair, and from the mass of yellow fur about her middle, and three little beetles with black and red markings scurried in terrified haste for cover, while Burl bore Saya to a resting-place of soft mold.

Burl was an ignorant savage, and to him Saya's deathlike unconsciousness was like death itself, but dumb misery smote him, and he laid her down gently, while tears came to his eyes and he called her name again and again in an agony of grief.

For an hour he sat there beside her, a man so lately pleased with himself above all creatures for having slain one huge beetle and put another to flight, as he would have looked upon it, now a broken-hearted, little pink-skinned man, weeping like a child, hunched up and bowed over with sorrow.

Then Saya slowly opened her eyes and stirred weakly.

THE FOREST OF DEATH

They were oblivious to everything but each other, Saya resting in still half-incredulous happiness against Burl's shoulder while he told her in little, jerky sentences of his pursuit of the colossal flying beetle, of his search for the tribe, and then his discovery of her apparently lifeless body.

When he spoke of the monster that had lurched from the mushroom thicket, and of the desperation with which he had faced it, Saya pressed close and looked at him with wondering and wonderful eyes. She could understand his willingness to die, believing her dead. A little while before she had felt the same indifference to life.

A timid, frightened whisper roused them from their absorption, and they looked up. One of the tribesmen stood upon one foot some distance away, staring at them, almost convinced that he looked upon the living dead. A sudden movement on the part of either of them would have sent him in a panic back into the mushroom forest. Two or three blond heads bobbed and vanished among the tangled stalks. Wide and astonished eyes gazed at the two they had believed the prey of malignant creatures.

The tribe had come slowly back to the mushroom they had been eating, leaderless, and convinced that Saya had fallen a victim to the deadly dust. Instead, they found her sitting by the side of their chief, apparently restored to them in some miraculous fashion.

Burl spoke, and the pink-skinned people came timorously from their hiding-places. They approached warily and formed a half-circle before the seated pair. Burl spoke again, and presently one of the bravest dared approach and touch him. Instantly a babble of the crude and labial language spoken by the tribe broke out. Awed questions and exclamations of thankfulness, then curious interrogations filled the air.

Burl, for once, showed some common sense. Instead of telling them in his usual vainglorious fashion of the adventures he had undergone, he merely cast down the two long and tapering antennæ from the flying beetle that he had torn from its dead body. They looked at them, and recognized their origin. Amazement and admiration showed upon their faces. Then Burl rose and abruptly ordered two of the men to make a chair of their hands for Saya. She was weak from the effects of the blow she had received. The two men humbly advanced and did as they were bid.

Then the march was taken up again, more slowly than before, because of Saya as a burden, but none the less steadily. Burl led his people across the country, marching in advance and with every nerve alert for signs of danger, but with more confidence and less timidity than he had ever displayed before.

All that noontime and that afternoon they filed steadily along, the tribesfolk keeping in a compact group close behind Burl. The man who had thrown away his spear had recovered it on an order from Burl, and the little party fairly bristled with weapons, though Burl knew well that they were liable to be cast away as impediments if flight should be necessary.

He was determined that his people should learn to fight the great creatures about them, instead of depending upon their legs for escape. He had led them in an attack upon great slugs, but they were defenseless creatures, incapable of more dangerous maneuvers than spasmodic jerkings of their great bodies.

The next time danger should threaten them, and especially if it came while their new awe of him held good, he was resolved to force them to join him in fighting it.

He had not long to wait for an opportunity to strengthen the spirit of his followers by a successful battle. The clouds toward the west were taking on a dull-red hue, which was the nearest to a sunset that was ever seen in the world of Burl's experience, when a bumble bee droned heavily over their heads, making for its hive.

The little group of people on the ground looked up and saw a scanty load of pollen packed in the stiff bristles of the insect's hind legs. The bees of the world had a hard time securing food upon the nearly flowerless planet, but this one had evidently made a find. Its crop was nearly filled with hard-gathered, viscous honey destined for the hival store.

It sped onward, heavily, its almost transparent wings mere blurs in the air from the rapidity of their vibration. Burl saw its many-faceted eyes staring before it in worried preoccupation as it soared in laborious speed over his head, some fifty feet up.

He dropped his glance, and then his eyes lighted with excitement. A slender-bodied wasp was shooting upward from an ambush it had found in a thicket of toadstools. It darted swiftly and gracefully upon the bee, which swerved and tried to flee. The droning buzz of the bee's wings rose to a higher note as it strove to increase its speed. The more delicately formed wasp headed the clumsier insect back.

The bee turned again and fled in terror. Each of the insects was slightly more than four feet in length, but the bee was much the heavier, and it could not attain the speed of which the wasp was capable.

The graceful form of the hunting insect rapidly overhauled its fleeing prey, and the wasp dashed in and closed with the bee at a point almost over the heads of the tribesmen. In a clawing, biting tangle of thrashing, transparent wings and black bodies, the two creatures tumbled to the earth. They fell perhaps thirty yards from where Burl stood watching.

Over and over the two insects rolled, now one uppermost, and then the other. The bee was struggling desperately to insert her sting in the more supple body of her adversary. She writhed and twisted, fighting with jaw and mandible, wing and claw.

The wasp was uppermost, and the bee lay on her back, fighting in panic-stricken desperation. The wasp saw an opening, her jaws darted in, and there was an instant of confusion. Then suddenly the bee, dazed, was upright with the wasp upon her. A movement too quick for the eye to follow—and the bee collapsed. The wasp had bitten her in the neck where all the nerve-cords passed, and the bee was dead.

Burl waited a moment more, aflame with excitement. He knew, as did all the tribefolk, what might happen next. When he saw the second act of the tragedy well begun, Burl snapped quick and harsh orders to his spear-armed men, and they followed him in a wavering line, their weapons tightly clutched.

Knowing the habits of the insects as they were forced to know them, they knew that the venture was one of the least dangerous they could undertake with fighting creatures the size of the wasp, but the idea of attacking the great creatures whose sharp stings could annihilate any of them with a touch, the mere thought of taking the initiative was appalling. Had their awe of Burl been less complete they would not have dreamed of following him.

PLANET NIGHTMARE

The second act of the tragedy had begun. The bee had been slain by the wasp, a carnivorous insect normally, but the wasp knew that sweet honey was concealed in the half-filled crop of the bee. Had the bee arrived safely at the hive, the sweet and sticky liquid would have been disgorged and added to the hival store. Now, though the bee's journey was ended and its flesh was to be crunched and devoured by the wasp, the honey was the first object of the pirate's solicitude. The dead insect was rolled over upon its back, and with eager haste the slayer began to exploit the body.

Burl and his men were creeping nearer, but with a gesture Burl bade them halt for a moment. The wasp's first move was to force the disgorgement of the honey from the bee's crop, and with feverish eagerness it pressed upon the limp body until the shining, sticky liquid appeared. Then the wasp began in ghoulish ecstasy to lick up the sweet stuff, utterly absorbed in the feast.

Many thousands of years before, the absorption of the then tiny insect had been noticed when engaged in a similar feat, and it was recorded in books moldered into dust long ages before Burl's birth that its rapture was so great that it had been known to fall a victim to a second bandit while engaged in the horrible banquet.

Burl had never read the books, but he had been told that the pirate would continue its feast even though seized by a greater enemy, unable to tear itself from the nectar gathered by the creature it had slain.

The tribesmen waited until the wasp had begun its orgy, licking up the toothsome stuff disgorged by its dead prey. It ate in gluttonous haste, blind to all sights, deaf to all sounds, able to think of nothing, conceive of nothing, but the delights of the liquid it was devouring.

At a signal the tribesmen darted forward. They wavered when near the slender-waisted gourmet, however, and Burl was the first to thrust his spear with all his strength into the thinly armored body.

Then the others took courage. A short, horny spear penetrated the very vitals of the wasp. A club fell with terrific impact upon the slender waist. There was a crackling, and the long, spidery limbs quivered and writhed, while the tribesmen fell back in fear, but without cause.

Burl struck again, and the wasp fell into two writhing halves, helpless for harm. The pink-skinned men danced in triumph, and the women and children ventured near, delighted.

Only Burl noticed that even as the wasp was dying, sundered and pierced with spears, its slender tongue licked out in one last, ecstatic taste of the nectar that had been its undoing.

Burdened with the pollen-covered legs of the giant bee, and filled with the meat from choice portions of the wasp's muscular limbs, the tribe resumed its journey. This time Burl had men behind him, still timid, still prone to flee at the slightest alarm, but infinitely more dependable than they had been before.

They had attacked and slain a wasp whose sting would have killed any of them. They had done battle under the leadership of Burl, whose spear had struck the first blow. Henceforth they were sharers, in a mild way, of his transcendent glory, and henceforth they were more like followers of a mighty chief and less like spineless worshipers of a demigod whose feats they were too timid to emulate.

That night they hid among a group of giant puff-balls, feasting on the loads of meat they had carried thus far with them. Burl watched them now without jealousy of their good spirits. He and Saya sat a little apart, happy to be near each other, speaking in low tones. After a time darkness fell, and the tribefolk became shapeless bodies speaking in voices that grew drowsy and were silent. The black forms of the toadstool heads and huge puff-balls were but darker against a dark sky.

The nightly rain began to fall, drop by drop, drop by drop, upon the damp and humid earth. Only Burl remained awake for a little while, and his last waking thought was of pride, disinterested pride. He had the first reward of the ruler, gratification in the greatness of his people.

The red mushrooms had continued to show their glistening heads, though Burl thought they were less numerous than in the territory from which the tribe had fled. All along the route, now to the right, now to the left, they had burst and sent their masses of deadly dust into the air.

Many times the tribefolk had been forced to make a detour to avoid a slowly spreading cloud of death-dealing spores. Once or twice their escapes had been narrow indeed, but so far there had been no deaths.

Burl had observed that the mushrooms normally burst only in the daytime, and for a while had thought of causing his followers to do their journeying in the night. Only the obvious disadvantages of such a course—the difficulty of discovering food, and the prowling spiders that roamed in the darkness—had prevented him. The idea still stayed with him, however, and two days after the fight with the hunting wasp he put it in practise.

The tribe came to the top of a small rise in the ground. For an hour they had been marching and counter-marching to avoid the suddenly appearing clouds of dust. Once they had been nearly hemmed in, and only by mad sprinting did they escape when three of the dull-red clouds seemed to flow together, closing three sides of a circle.

They came to the little hillock and halted. Before them stretched a plain all of four miles wide, colored a brownish brick-red by masses of mushrooms. They had seen mushroom forests before, and knew of the dangers they presented, but there was none so deadly as the plain before them. To right and left it stretched as far as the eye could see, but far away on its farther edge Burl caught a glimpse of flowing water.

Over the plain itself a dull-red haze seemed to float. It was nothing more or less than a cloud of the deadly spores, dispersed and indefinite, constantly replenished by the freshly bursting red mushrooms.

While the people stood and watched a dozen thick columns of dust rose into the air from scattered points here and there upon the plain, settling slowly again, but leaving behind them enough of their finely divided substance to keep the thin red haze over the whole plain in its original, deadly state.

Burl had seen single red mushrooms before, and even small thickets of two and three, but here was a plain of millions, literally millions upon millions of the malignant growths. Here was one fungoid forest through whose aisles no monster beetles stalked, and above whose shadowed depths no brightly colored butterflies fluttered in joyous abandon. There were no loud-voiced crickets singing in its hiding-places, nor bodies of eagerly foraging ants searching inquisitively for bits of food. It was a forest of death, still and silent, quiet and motionless save for the sullen columns of red dust that ever and again shot upward from the torn and ragged envelope of the bursting mushroom.

Burl and his people watched in wonderment and dismay, but presently a high resolve came to Burl. The mushrooms never burst at night, and the deadly dust from a subsided cloud was not deadly in the morning. As a matter of fact the rain that fell every night made it no more than a sodden, thin film of reddish mud by daybreak, mud which dried and caked.

Burl did not know what occurred, but knew the result. At night or in early morning, the danger from the red mushrooms was slight. Therefore he would lead his people through the very jaws of death that night. He would lead them through the deadly aisles of this, the forest of malignant growths, the place of lurking annihilation.

It was an act of desperation, and the resolution to carry it through left Burl in a state of mind that kept him from observing one thing that would have ended all the struggles of his tribe at once. Perhaps a quarter-mile from the edge of the red forest three or four giant cabbages grew, thrusting their colossal leaves upward toward the sky.

And on the cabbages a dozen lazy slugs fed leisurely, ignoring completely the red haze that was never far from them and sometimes covered them. Burl saw them, but the oddity of their immunity from the effects of the red dust did not strike him. He was fighting to keep his resolution intact. If he had only realized the significance of what he saw, however—

The slugs were covered with a thick soft fur. The tribespeople wore garments of that same material. The fur protected the slugs, and could have made the tribe immune to the deadly red dust if they had only known. The slugs breathed through a row of tiny holes upon their backs, as the mature insects breathed through holes upon the bottom of their abdomens, and the soft fur formed a mat of felt which arrested the fine particles of deadly dust, while allowing the pure air to pass through. It formed, in effect, a natural gas-mask which the tribesmen should have adopted, but which they did not discover or invent.

The remainder of that day they waited in a curious mixture of resolve and fear. The tribe was rapidly reaching a point where it would follow Burl over a thousand-foot cliff, and it needed some such blind confidence to make them prepare to go through the forest of the million deadly mushrooms.

The waiting was a strain, but the actual journey was a nightmare. Burl knew that the toadstools did not burst of themselves during the night, but he knew that the beetle on which he had taken his involuntary ride had crashed against one in the darkness, and that the fatal dust had poured out. He warned his people to be cautious, and led them down the slope of the hill through the blackness.

PLANET NIGHTMARE

For hours they stumbled on in utter darkness, with the pungent, acrid odor of the red growths constantly in their nostrils. They put out their hands and touched the flabby, damp stalks of the monstrous things. They stumbled and staggered against the leathery skins of the malignant fungoids.

Death was all about them. At no time during all the dark hours of the night was there a moment when they could not reach out their hands and touch a fungus growth that might burst at their touch and fill the air with poisonous dust, so that all of them would die in gasping, choking agony.

And worst of all, before half an hour was past they had lost all sense of direction, so that they stumbled on blindly through the utter blackness, not knowing whether they were headed toward the river that might be their salvation or were wandering hopelessly deeper and deeper into the silent depths of the forest of strangled things.

When day came again and the mushrooms sent their columns of fatal dust into the air would they gasp and fight for breath in the red haze that would float like a tenuous cloud above the forest? Would they breathe in flames of firelike torment and die slowly, or would the red dust be merciful and slay them quickly?

They felt their way like blind folk, devoid of hope and curiously unafraid. Only their hearts were like heavy, cold weights in their breasts, and they shouldered aside the swollen sacs of the red mushrooms with a singular apathy as they followed Burl slowly through the midst of death.

Many times in their journeying they knew that dead creatures were near by—moths, perhaps, that had blundered into a distended growth which had burst upon the impact and killed the thing that had touched it.

No busy insect scavengers ventured into this plain of silence to salvage the bodies, however. The red haze preserved the sanctuary of malignance inviolate. During the day no creature might hope to approach its red aisles and dust-carpeted clearings, and at night the slow-dropping rain fell only upon the rounded heads of the mushrooms.

In all the space of the forest, only the little band of hopeless people, plodding on behind Burl in the velvet blackness, callously rubbed shoulders with death in the form of the red and glistening mushrooms. Over all the dank expanse of the forest, the only sound was the dripping of the slow and sodden rainfall that began at nightfall and lasted until day came again.

The sky began to grow faintly gray as the sun rose behind the banks of overhanging clouds. Burl stopped short and uttered what was no more than a groan. He was in a little circular clearing, and the twisted, monstrous forms of the deadly mushrooms were all about. There was not yet enough light for colors to appear, and the hideous, almost obscene shapes of the loathsome growths on every side showed only as mocking, leering silhouettes as of malicious demons rejoicing at the coming doom of the gray-faced, huddled tribefolk.

Burl stood still, drooping in discouragement upon his spear, the feathery moth's antennæ bound upon his forehead shadowed darkly against the graying sky. Soon the mushrooms would begin to burst—

Then, suddenly, he lifted his head, encouragement and delight upon his features. He had heard the ripple of running water. His followers looked at him with dawning hope. Without a word, Burl began to run, and they followed him more slowly. His voice came back to them in a shout of delight.

Then they, too, broke into a jog-trot. In a moment they had emerged from the thick tangle of brownish-red stalks and were upon the banks of a wide and swiftly running river, the same river whose gleam Burl had caught the day before from the farther side of the mushroom forest.

Once before Burl had floated down a river upon a mushroom raft. Then his journey had been involuntary and unlooked for. He had been carried far from his tribe and far from Saya, and his heart had been filled with desolation.

Now he viewed the swiftly running current with eager delight. He cast his eyes up and down the bank. Here and there the river-bank rose in a low bluff, and thick shelf-growths stretched out above the water.

Burl was busy in an instant, stabbing the hard growths with his spear and striving to wrench them free. The tribesmen stared at him, uncomprehending, but at an order from him they did likewise.

Soon a dozen thick masses of firm, light fungus lay upon the shore where it shelved gently into the water. Burl began to explain what they were to do, but one or two of the men dared remonstrate, saying humbly that they were afraid to part from him. If they might embark upon the same thing with him, they would be safe, but otherwise they were afraid.

Burl cast an apprehensive glance at the sky. Day was coming rapidly on.

PLANET NIGHTMARE

Soon the red mushrooms would begin to shoot their columns of deadly dust into the air. This was no time to pause and deliberate. Then Saya spoke softly.

Burl listened, and made a mighty sacrifice. He took his gorgeous velvet cloak from his shoulders—it was made from the wing of a great moth—and tore it into a dozen long, irregular pieces, tearing it along the lines of the sinews that reinforced it. He planted his spear upright in the largest piece of shelf-fungus and caused his followers to do likewise, then fastened the strips of sinew and velvet to his spear-shaft, and ordered them to do the same to the other spears.

In a matter of minutes the dozen tiny rafts were bobbing on the water, clustered about the larger, central bit. Then, one by one, the tribefolk took their places, and Burl shoved off.

The agglomeration of cranky, unseaworthy bits of shelf-fungus moved slowly out from the shore until the current caught it. Burl and Saya sat upon the central bit, with the other trustful but somewhat frightened pink-skinned people all about them. And, as they began to move between the mushroom-lined banks of the river and the mist of the night began to lift from its surface, far in the interior of the forest of the red fungoids a column of sullen red leaped into the air. The first of the malignant growths had cast its cargo of poisonous dust into the still-humid atmosphere.

The conelike column spread out and grew thin, but even after it had sunk into the earth, a reddish taint remained in the air about the place where it had been. The deadly red haze that hung all through the day over the red forest was in process of formation.

But by that time the unstable fungus rafts were far down the river, bobbing and twirling in the current, with the wide-eyed people upon them gazing in wonderment at the shores as they glided by. The red mushrooms grew less numerous upon the banks. Other growths took their places. Molds and rusts covered the ground as grass had done in ages past. Mushrooms showed their creamy, rounded heads. Malformed things with swollen trunks and branches in strange mockery of the trees they had superseded made their appearance, and once the tribesmen saw the dark bulk of a hunting spider outlined for a moment upon the bank.

All the long day they rode upon the current, while the insect life that had been absent in the neighborhood of the forest of death made its appearance again. Bees once more droned overhead, and wasps and dragon-flies. Four-inch mosquitoes made their appearance, to be fought off by the tribefolk with lusty blows, and glittering beetles and shining flies, whose bodies glittered with a metallic luster, buzzed and flew above the water.

Huge butterflies once more were seen, dancing above the steaming, festering earth in an apparent ecstasy from the mere fact of existence, and all the thousand and one forms of insect life that flew and crawled, and swam and dived, showed themselves to the tribesmen on the raft.

Water-beetles came lazily to the surface, to snap with sudden energy at mosquitoes busily laying their eggs in the nearly stagnant water by the river-banks. Burl pointed out to Saya, with some excitement, their silver breast-plates that shone as they darted under the water again. And the shell-covered boats of a thousand caddis-worms floated in the eddies and back-waters of the stream. Water-boatmen and whirligigs—almost alone among insects in not having shared in the general increase of size—danced upon the oily waves.

The day wore on as the shores flowed by. The tribefolk ate of their burdens of mushroom and meat, and drank from the fresh water of the river. Then, when afternoon came, the character of the country about the stream changed. The banks fell away, and the current slackened. The shores became indefinite, and the river merged itself into a swamp, a vast swamp from which a continual muttering came which the tribesmen heard for a long time before they saw the swamp itself.

The water seemed to turn dark, as black mud took the place of the clay that had formed its bed, and slowly, here and there, then more frequently, floating green things that were stationary, and did not move with the current, appeared. They were the leaves of water-lilies, that had remained with the giant cabbages and a very few other plants in the midst of a fungoid world. The green leaves were twelve feet across, and any one of them would have floated the whole of Burl's tribe.

Presently they grew numerous so that the channel was made narrow, and the mushroom rafts passed between rows of the great leaves, with here and there a colossal, waxen blossom in which three men might have hidden and which exhaled an almost over-powering fragrance into the air.

And the muttering that had been heard far away grew in volume to an intermittent, incredibly deep bass roar. It seemed to come from the banks on either side, and actually was the discordant croaking of the giant frogs, grown to eight feet in length, which lived and loved in the huge swamp, above which golden butterflies danced in ecstasy, and which the transcendently beautiful blossoms of the water-lilies filled with fragrance.

The swamp was a place of riotous life. The green bodies of the colossal frogs—perched upon the banks in strange immobility and only opening their huge mouths to emit their thunderous croakings—the green bodies of the frogs blended queerly with the vivid color of the water-lily leaves. Dragon-flies fluttered in their swift and angular flight above the black and reeking mud. Green-bottles and blue-bottles and a hundred other species of flies buzzed busily in the misty air, now and then falling prey to the licking tongues of the frogs.

Bees droned overhead in flight less preoccupied and worried than elsewhere flitting from blossom to blossom of the tremendous water-lilies, loading their crops with honey and the bristles of their legs with yellow pollen.

Everywhere over the mushroom-covered world the air was never quite free from mist, and the steaming exhalations of the pools, but here in the swamps the atmosphere was so heavily laden with moisture that the bodies of the tribefolk were covered with glistening droplets, while the wide, flat water-lily leaves glittered like platters of jewels from the "steam" that had condensed upon their upper surfaces.

The air was full of shining bodies and iridescent wings. Myriads of tiny midges—no more than three or four inches across their wings—danced above the slow-flowing water. And butterflies of every imaginable shade and color, from the most delicate lavender to the most vivid carmine, danced and fluttered, alighting upon the white water-lilies to sip daintily of their nectar, skimming the surface of the water, enamored of their brightly tinted reflections.

And the pink-skinned tribesfolk, floating through this fairyland on their mushroom rafts, gazed with wide eyes at the beauty about them, and drew in great breaths of the intoxicating fragrance of the great white flowers that floated like elfin boats upon the dark water.

MURRAY LEINSTER

OUT OF BONDAGE

The mist was heavy and thick, and through it the flying creatures darted upon their innumerable businesses, visible for an instant in all their colorful beauty, then melting slowly into indefiniteness as they sped away. The tribefolk on the clustered rafts watched them as they darted overhead, and for hours the little squadron of fungoid vessels floated slowly through the central channel of the marsh.

The river had split into innumerable currents which meandered purposelessly through the glistening black mud of the swamp, but after a long time they seemed to reassemble, and Burl could see what had caused the vast morass.

Hills appeared on either side of the stream, which grew higher and steeper, as if the foothills of a mountain chain. Then Burl turned and peered before him.

Rising straight from the low hills, a wall of high mountains rose toward the sky, and the low-hanging clouds met their rugged flanks but half-way toward the peaks. To right and left the mountains melted into the tenuous haze, but ahead they were firm and stalwart, rising and losing their heights in the cloud-banks.

They formed a rampart which might have guarded the edge of the world, and the river flowed more and more rapidly in a deeper and narrower current toward a cleft between two rugged giants that promised to swallow the water and all that might swim in its depths or float upon its surface.

Tall, steep hills rose from either side of the swift current, their sides covered with flaking molds of an exotic shade of rose-pink, mingled here and there with lavender and purple. Rocks, not hidden beneath a coating of fungus, protruded their angular heads from the hillsides. The river valley became a gorge, and then little more than a cañon, with beetling sides that frowned down upon the swift current running beneath them.

The small flotilla passed beneath an overhanging cliff, and then shot out to where the cliffsides drew apart and formed a deep amphitheater, whose top was hidden in the clouds.

And across this open space, on cables all of five hundred feet long, a banded spider had flung its web. It was a monster of its tribe. Its belly was swollen to a diameter of no less than two yards, and its outstretched legs would have touched eight points of a ten-yard circle.

105

PLANET NIGHTMARE

It was hanging motionless in the center of the colossal snare as the little group of tribefolk passed underneath, and they saw the broad bands of yellow and black and silver upon its abdomen. They shivered as their little crafts were swept below.

Then they came to a little valley, where yellow sand bordered the river and there was a level space of a hundred yards on either side before the steep sides of the mountains began their rise. Here the cluster of mushroom rafts were caught in a little eddy and drawn out of the swiftly flowing current. Soon there was a soft and yielding jar. The rafts had grounded.

Led by Burl, the tribesmen waded ashore, wonderment and excitement in their hearts. Burl searched all about with his eyes. Toadstools and mushrooms, rusts and molds, even giant puff-balls grew in the little valley, but of the deadly red mushrooms he saw none.

A single bee was buzzing slowly over the tangled thickets of fungoids, and the loud voice of a cricket came in a deafening burst of sound, reechoed from the hillsides, but save for the far-flung web of the banded spider a mile or more away, there was no sign of the deadly creatures that preyed upon men.

Burl began to climb the hillside with his tribefolk after him. For an hour they toiled upward, through confused masses of fungus of almost every species. Twice they stopped to seize upon edible fungi and break them into masses they could carry, and once they paused and made a wide detour around a thicket from which there came a stealthy rustling.

Burl believed that the rustling was merely the sound of a moth or butterfly emerging from its chrysalis, but was unwilling to take any chances. He and his people circled the mushroom thicket and mounted higher.

And at last, perhaps six or seven hundred feet above the level of the river, they came upon a little plateau, going back into a small pocket in the mountainside. Here they found many of the edible fungoids, and no less than a dozen of the giant cabbages, on whose broad leaves many furry grubs were feeding steadily in placid contentment with themselves and all the world.

A small stream bubbled up from a tiny basin and ran swiftly across the plateau, and there were dense thickets of toadstools in which the tribesmen might find secure hiding-places. The tribe would make itself a new home here.

That night they hid among inextricably tangled masses of mushrooms, and saw with amazement the multitude of creatures that ventured forth in the darkness. All the valley and the plateau were illumined by the shining beacons of huge but graceful fireflies, who darted here and there in delight and—apparently—in security.

Upon the earth below, also, many tiny lights glowed. The larvæ of the fireflies crawled slowly but happily over the fungus-covered mountainside, and great glow-worms clambered upon the shining tops of the toadstools and rested there, twin broad bands of bluish fire burning brightly within their translucent bodies.

They were the females of the firefly race, which never attain to legs and wings, but crawl always upon the earth, merely enlarged creatures in the forms of their own larvæ. Moths soared overhead with mighty, throbbing wing-beats, and all the world seemed a paradise through which no evil creatures roamed in search of prey.

And a strange thing came to pass. Soon after darkness fell upon the earth and the steady drip-drop of the rain began, a musical tinkling sound was heard which grew in volume, and became a deep-toned roar, which reechoed and reverberated from the opposite hillsides until it was like melodious and long-continued thunder. For a long time the people were puzzled and a little afraid, but Burl took courage and investigated.

He emerged from the concealing thicket and peered cautiously about, seeing nothing. Then he dared move in the direction of the sound, and the gleam from a dozen fireflies showed him a sheet of water pouring over a vertical cliff to the river far below.

The rainfall, gentle as it was, when gathered from all the broad expanse of the mountainside, made a river of its own, which had scoured out a bed, and poured down each night to plunge in a smother of spray and foam through six hundred feet of empty space to the swiftly flowing river in the center of the valley. It was this sound that had puzzled the tribefolk, and this sound that lulled them to sleep when Burl at last came back to allay their fears.

The next day they explored their new territory with a boldness of which they would not have been capable a month before. They found a single great trap-door in the earth, sure sign of the burrow of a monster spider, and Burl resolved that before many days the spider would be dealt with. He told his tribesmen so, and they nodded their heads solemnly instead of shrinking back in terror as they would have done not long since.

The tribe was rapidly becoming a group of men, capable of taking the aggressive. They needed Burl's rash leadership, and for many generations they would need bold leaders, but they were infinitely superior to the timid, rabbit-like creatures they had been. They bore spears, and they had used them. They had seen danger, and had blindly followed Burl through the forest of strangled things instead of fleeing weakly from the peril.

They wore soft, yellow fur about their middles, taken from the bodies of giant slugs they had slain. They had eaten much meat, and preferred its succulent taste to the insipid savor of the mushrooms that had once been their steady diet. They knew the exhilaration of brave adventure—though they had been forced into adventure by Burl—and they were far more worthy descendants of their ancestors than those ancestors had known for many thousand years.

The exploration of their new domain yielded many wonders and a few advantages. The tribefolk found that the nearest ant-city was miles away, and that the small insects would trouble them but rarely. (The nightly rush of water down the sloping sides of the mountain made it undesirable for the site of an ant colony.)

And best of all, back in the little pocket in the mountainside, they found old and disused cells of hunting wasps. The walls of the pocket were made of soft sandstone with alternate layers of clay, and the wasps had found digging easy.

There were a dozen or more burrows, the shaft of each some four feet in diameter and going back into the cliff for nearly thirty feet, where they branched out into a number of cells. Each of the cells had once held a grub which had grown fat and large upon its hoard of paralyzed crickets, and then had broken away to the outer world to emerge as a full-grown wasp.

Now, however, the laboriously tunneled caverns would furnish a hiding-place for the tribe of men, a far more secure hiding-place than the center of the mushroom thickets. And, furthermore, a hiding-place which, because more permanent, would gradually become a possession for which the men would fight.

It is a curious thing that the advancement of a people from a state of savagery and continual warfare to civilization and continual peace is not made by the elimination of the causes of strife, but by the addition of new objects and ideals, in defense of which that same people will offer battle.

A single chrysalis was found securely anchored to the underside of a rock-shelf, and Burl detached it with great labor and carried it into one of the burrows, though the task was one that was almost beyond his strength. He desired the butterfly that would emerge for his own use.

He preempted, too, a solitary burrow a little distant from the others, and made preparations for an event that was destined to make his plans wiser and more far-reaching than before.

His followers were equally busy with their various burrows, gathering stores of soft growth for their couches, and later—at Burl's suggestion—even carrying within the dark caverns the radiant heads of the luminous mushrooms to furnish illumination. The light would be dim, and after the mushroom had partly dried it would cease, but for a people utterly ignorant of fire it was far from a bad plan.

Burl was very happy for that time. His people looked upon him as a savior, and obeyed his least order without question. He was growing to repose some measure of trust in them, too, as men who began to have some glimmerings of the new-found courage that had come to him, and which he had striven hard to implant in their breasts.

The tribe had been a formless gathering of people. There were six or seven men and as many women, and naturally families had come into being—sometimes after fierce and absurd fights among the men—but the families were not the sharply distinct agreements they would have been in a tribe of higher development.

The marriage was but an agreement, terminable at any time, and the men had but little of the feeling of parenthood, though the women had all the fierce maternal instinct of the insects about them.

These burrows in which the tribefolk were making their homes would put an end to the casual nature of the marriage bonds. They were homes in the making—damp and humid burrows without fire or heat, but homes, nevertheless. The family may come before the home, in the development of mankind, but it invariably exists when the home has been made.

The tribe had been upon the plateau for nearly a week when Burl found that stirrings and strugglings were going on within the huge cocoon he had laid close beside the burrow he had chosen for his own. He cast aside all other work, and waited patiently for the thing he knew was about to happen. He squatted on his haunches beside the huge, oblong cylinder, his spear in his hand, waiting patiently. From time to time he nibbled at a bit of edible mushroom.

Burl had acquired many new traits, among which a little foresight was most prominent, but he had never conquered the habit of feeling hungry at any and every time that food was near at hand. He had to wait. He had food. Therefore, he ate.

The sound of scrapings came from the closed cocoon, caked upon its outer side with dirt and mold. The scraping and scratching continued, and presently a tiny hole showed, which rapidly enlarged. Tiny jaws and a dry, glazed skin became visible, the skin looking as if it had been varnished with many coats of brown shellac. Then a malformed head forced its way through and stopped.

All motion ceased for a matter of perhaps half an hour, and then the strange, blind head seemed to become distended, to be swelling. A crack appeared along its upper part, which lengthened and grew wide. And then a second head appeared from within the first.

This head was soft and downy, and a slender proboscis was coiled beneath its lower edge like the trunk of one of the elephants that had been extinct for many thousand years. Soft scales and fine hairs alternated to cover it, and two immense, many-faceted eyes gazed mildly at the world on which it was looking for the first time. The color of the whole was purest milky-white.

Slowly and painfully, assisting itself by slender, colorless legs that seemed strangely feeble and trembling, a butterfly crawled from the cocoon. Its wings were folded and lifeless, without substance or color, but the body was a perfect white. The butterfly moved a little distance from its cocoon and slowly unfurled its wings. With the action, life seemed to be pumped into them from some hidden spring in the insect's body. The slender antennæ spread out and wavered gently in the warm air. The wings were becoming broad expanses of snowy velvet.

A trace of eagerness seemed to come into the butterfly's actions. Somewhere there in the valley sweet food and joyous companions awaited it. Fluttering above the fungoids of the hillsides, surely there was a mate with whom the joys of love were to be shared, surely upon those gigantic patches of green, half hidden in the haze, there would be laid tiny golden eggs that in time would hatch into small, fat grubs.

Strength came to the butterfly's limbs. Its wings were spread and closed with a new assurance. It spread them once more, and raised them to make the first flight of this new existence in a marvelous world, full of delights and adventures—Burl struck home with his spear.

The delicate limbs struggled in agony, the wings fluttered helplessly, and in a little while the butterfly lay still upon the fungus-carpeted earth, and Burl leaned over to strip away the great wings of snow-white velvet, to sever the long and slender antennæ, and then to call his tribesmen and bid them share in the food he had for them.

And there was a feast that afternoon. The tribesmen sat about the white carcass, cracking open the delicate limbs for the meat within them, and Burl made sure that Saya secured the choicest bits. The tribesmen were happy. Then one of the children of the tribe stretched a hand aloft and pointed up the mountainside.

Coming slowly down the slanting earth was a long, narrow file of living animals. For a time the file seemed to be but one creature, but Burl's keen eyes soon saw that there were many. They were caterpillars, each one perhaps ten feet long, each with a tiny black head armed with sharp jaws, and with dull-red fur upon their backs. The rear of the procession was lost in the mist of the low-hanging cloud-banks that covered the mountainside some two thousand feet above the plateau, but the foremost was no more than three hundred yards away.

Slowly and solemnly the procession came on, the black head of the second touching the rear of the first, and the head of the third touching the rear of the second. In faultless alignment, without intervals, they moved steadily down the slanting side of the mountain.

Save the first, they seemed absorbed in maintaining their perfect formation, but the leader constantly rose upon his hinder half and waved the fore part of his body in the air, first to the right and then to the left, as if searching out the path he would follow.

The tribefolk watched in amazement mingled with terror. Only Burl was calm. He had never seen a slug that meant danger to man, and he reasoned that these were at any rate moving slowly so that they could be distanced by the fleeter-footed human beings, but he also meant to be cautious.

The slow march kept on. The rear of the procession of caterpillars emerged from the cloud-bank, and Burl saw that a shining white line was left behind them. No less than eighty great caterpillars clad in white and dingy red were solemnly moving down the mountainside, leaving a path of shining silk behind them. Head to tail, in single file, they had no eyes or ears for anything but their procession.

The leader reached the plateau, and turned. He came to the cluster of giant cabbages, and ignored them. He came to a thicket of mushrooms, and passed through it, followed by his devoted band. Then he came to an open space where the earth was soft and sandy, where sandstone had weathered and made a great heap of easily moved earth.

The leading caterpillar halted, and began to burrow experimentally in the ground. The result pleased him, and some signal seemed to pass along the eight-hundred-foot line of creatures. The leader began to dig with feet and jaws, working furiously to cover himself completely with the soft earth. Those immediately behind him abandoned their formation, and pressed forward in haste. Those still farther back moved more hurriedly.

All, when they reached the spot selected by the leader, abandoned any attempt to keep to their line, and hastened to find an unoccupied spot in the open space in which to bury themselves.

For perhaps half an hour the clearing was the scene of intense activity, incredible activity. Huge, ten-foot bodies burrowed desperately in the whitish earth, digging frantically to cover themselves.

After the half-hour, however, the last of the caterpillars had vanished. Only an occasional movement of the earth from the struggle of a buried creature to bury itself still deeper, and the freshly turned surface showed that beneath the clearing on the plateau eighty great slugs were preparing themselves for the sleep of metamorphosis. The piled-up earth and the broad, white band of silk, leading back up the hillside until it became lost in the clouds, alone remained to tell of the visitation.

The tribesmen had watched in amazement. They had never seen these creatures before, but they knew, of course, why they had entombed themselves. Had they known what the scientists of thirty thousand years before had written in weighty and dull books, they would have deduced from the appearance of the processionary caterpillars—or pine-caterpillars—that somewhere above the banks of clouds there were growing trees and sunlight, that a moon shone down, and stars twinkled from the blue vault of a cloudless sky.

But the tribesmen did not know. They only knew that there, beneath the soft earth, was a mighty store of food for them when they cared to dig for it, that their provisions for many months were secure, and that Burl, their leader, was a great and mighty man for having led them to this land of safety and plenty.

Burl read their emotions in their eyes, but better than their amazement and wonderment was a glance that had nothing whatever to do with his leadership of the tribe. And then Burl rose, and took the two snowy-white velvet cloaks from the wings of the white butterfly. One of them he flung about his own shoulders, and the other he flung about Saya. And then those two stood up before the wide-eyed tribesmen, and Burl spoke:

"This is my mate, and my food is her food, and her wrath is my wrath. My burrow is her burrow, and her sorrow, my sorrow.

"Men whom I have led to this land of plenty, hear me. As ye obey my words, see to it that the words of Saya are obeyed likewise, for my spear will loose the life from any man who angers her. Know that as I am great beyond all other men, so Saya is great beyond all other women, for I say it, and it is so."

And he drew Saya toward him, trembling slightly, and put his arm about her waist before all the tribe, and the tribesmen muttered in acquiescent whispers that what Burl said was true, as they had already known.

Then, while the pink-skinned men feasted on the meat Burl had provided for them, he and Saya went toward the burrow he had made ready. It was not like the other burrows, being set apart from them, and its entrance was bordered on either side by mushrooms as black as night. All about the entrance the black mushrooms clustered, a strange species that grew large and scattered its spores abroad and then of its own accord melted into an inky liquid that flowed away, sinking slowly into the ground.

In a little hollow below the opening of the burrow an inky pool had gathered, which reflected the gray clouds above and the shapes of the mushrooms that overhung its edges.

Burl and Saya made their way toward the burrow in silence, a picturesque couple against the black background of the sable mushrooms and the earth made dark by the inky liquid. Both of their figures were swathed in cloaks of unsmirched whiteness and wondrous softness, and bound to Burl's forehead were the feathery, lacelike antenna of a great moth, making flowing plumes of purest gold. His spear seemed cast from bronze, and he was a proud figure as he led Saya past the black pool and to the doorway of their home.

They sat there, watching, while the darkness came on and the moths and fireflies emerged to dance in the night, and listened when the rain began its slow, deliberate dripping from the heavy clouds above. Presently a gentle rumbling began—the accumulation of the rain from all the mountainside forming a torrent that would pour in a six-hundred-foot drop to the river far below.

The sound of the rushing water grew louder, and was echoed back from the cliffs on the other side of the valley. The fireflies danced like fairy lights in the chasm, and all the creatures of the night winged their way aloft to join in the ecstasy of life and love.

And then, when darkness was complete, and only the fitful gleams of the huge fireflies were reflected from the still surface of the black pool beneath their feet, Burl reached out his hand to Saya, sitting beside him in the darkness. She yielded shyly, and her soft, warm hand found his in the obscurity. And Burl bent over and kissed her on the lips.

NIGHTMARE PLANET

The Directory-ship *Tethys* made the first landing on the planet, L216[12]. It was a goodly world, with an ample atmosphere and many seas, which the nearby sun warmed so lavishly that a perpetual cloud-bank hid them and all the solid ground from view. It had mountains and islands and high plateaus. It had day and night and rain. It had an equable climate, rather on the tropical side. But it possessed no life.

No animals roamed its solid surface. No vegetation grew from its rocks. Not even bacteria struggled with the stones to turn them into soil. No living thing, however small, swam in its oceans. It was one of that disappointing vast majority of otherwise admirable worlds which was unsuited for colonization solely because it had not been colonized before. It could be used for biological experiments in a completely germ-free environment, or ships could land upon it for water and supplies of air. The water was pure and the air breathable, but it had no other present utility. Such was the case with an overwhelming number of Earth-type planets when first discovered in the exploration of the galaxy. Life simply hadn't started there.

So the ship which first landed upon it made due note for the Galactic Directory and went away, and no other ship came near the planet for eight hundred years.

But nearly a millennium later, the Seed-Ship *Orana* arrived. It landed and carefully seeded the useless world. It circled endlessly above the clouds, dribbling out a fine dust comprised of the spores of every conceivable microorganism that could break down rock to powder and turn the powder to organic matter. It also seeded with moulds and fungi and lichens, and everything that could turn powdery primitive soil into stuff on which higher forms of life could grow. The *Orana* seeded the seas with plankton. Then it, too, went away.

Centuries passed. Then the Ecological Preparation Ship *Ludred* swam to the planet from space. It was a gigantic ship of highly improbable construction and purpose. It found the previous seeding successful. Now there was soil which swarmed with minute living things. There were fungi which throve monstrously. The seas stank of teeming minuscule life-forms. There were even some novelties on land, developed by strictly local conditions. There were, for example, *paramecium* as big as grapes, and yeasts had increased in size so that they bore flowers visible to the naked eye. The life on the planet was not aboriginal, though. It had all been planted by the seed-ship of centuries before.

The *Ludred* released insects, it dumped fish into the seas. It scattered plant-seeds over the continents. It treated the planet to a sort of Russell's Mixture of living things. The real Russell's Mixture is that blend of simple elements in the proportions found in suns. This was a blend of living creatures, of whom some should certainly survive by consuming the now habituated flora, and others which should survive by preying on the first. The planet was stocked, in effect, with everything it could be hoped might live there.

But at the time of the *Ludred's* visit of course no creature needing parental care had any chance of survival. Everything had to be able to care for itself the instant it burst its egg. So there were no birds or mammals. Trees and plants of divers sorts, and fish and crustaceans and insects could be planted. Nothing else.

The *Ludred* swam away through emptiness.

There should have been another planting, centuries later still, but it was never made. When the Ecological Preparation Service was moved to Algol IV, a file was upset. The cards in it were picked up and replaced, but one was missed. So that planet was forgotten. It circled its sun in emptiness. Cloud-banks covered it from pole to pole. There were hazy markings in certain places, where high plateaus penetrated the clouds. But from space the planet was featureless. Seen from afar, it was merely a round white ball—white from its cloud-banks and nothing else.

But on its surface, in its lowlands it was nightmare.

Especially was it nightmare—after some centuries—for the descendants of the human beings from the space-liner *Icarus*, wrecked there some forty-odd generations ago. Naturally, nobody anywhere else thought of the *Icarus* any more. It was not even remembered by the descendants of its human cargo, who now inhabited the planet. The wreckage of the ship was long since hidden under the seething, furiously striving fungi of the boil. The human beings on the planet had forgotten not only the ship but very nearly everything—how they came to this world, the use of metals, the existence of fire, and even the fact that there was such a thing as sunlight. They lived in the lowlands, deep under the cloud-bank, amid surroundings which were riotous, swarming, frenzied horror. They had become savages. They were less than savages. They had forgotten their high destiny as men.

*

Dawn came. Grayness appeared overhead and increased. That was all. The sky was a blank, colorless pall, merely mottled where the clouds clustered a little thicker or a little thinner, as clouds do. But the landscape was variegated enough! Where the little group of people huddled together, there was a wide valley. Its walls rose up and up into the very clouds. The people had never climbed those hillsides.

They had not even traditions of what might lie above them, and their lives had been much too occupied to allow of speculations on cosmology. By day they were utterly absorbed in two problems which filled every waking minute. One was the securing of food to eat, under the conditions of the second problem, which was that of merely staying alive.

There was only one of their number who sometimes thought of other matters, and he did so because he had become lost from his group of humans once, and had found his way back to it. His name was Burl, and his becoming lost was pure fantastic accident, and his utilization of a fully inherited power to think was the result of extraordinary events. But he still had not the actual habit of thinking. This morning he was like his fellows.

All of them were soaked with wetness. During the night—every night—the sky dripped slow, spaced, solemn water-drops during the whole of the dark hours. This was customary. But normally the humans hid in the mushroom-forests, sheltered by the toadstools which now grew to three man-heights. They denned in small openings in the tangled mass of parasitic growths which flourished in such thickets. But this last night they had camped in the open. They had no proper habitations of their own. Caves would have been desirable, but insects made use of caves, and the descendants of insects introduced untold centuries before had shared in the size-increase of *paramecium* and yeasts and the few true plants which had been able to hold their own. Mining-wasps were two yards long, and bumble-bees were nearly as huge, and there were other armored monstrosities which also preferred caves for their own purposes. And of course the humans could not build habitations, because anything men built to serve the purpose of a cave would instantly be preempted by creatures who would automatically destroy any previous occupants.

PLANET NIGHTMARE

The humans had no fixed dens at any time. Now they had not even shelter. They lacked other things, also. They had no tools save salvaged scraps of insect-armor—great sawtoothed mandibles or razor-pointed leg-shells—which they used to pry apart the edible fungi on which they lived, or to get at the morsels of meat left behind when the brainless lords of this planet devoured each other. They had not even any useful knowledge, except desperately accurate special knowledge of the manners and customs of the insects they could not defy. And on this special morning they concluded that they were doomed. They were going to be killed. They stood shivering in the open, waiting for it to happen.

It was not exactly news. They had had warning days ago, but they could do nothing about it. Their home valley, to be sure, would have made any civilized human being shudder merely to look at it, but they had considered it almost paradise. It was many miles long, and a fair number wide, and a stream ran down its middle. At the lower end of the valley there was a vast swamp, from which at nightfall the thunderously deep-bass croaking of giant frogs could be heard. But that swamp had kept out the more terrifying creatures of that world. The thirty-foot centipedes could not cross it or did not choose to. The mastodon-sized tarantulas which ravaged so much of the planet would not cross it save in pursuit of prey. So the valley was nearly a haven of safety.

True, there was one clotho spider in its ogre's castle nearby, and there was a labyrinth spider in a minor valley which nobody had ever ventured into, and there were some—not many—praying-mantises as tall as giraffes. They wandered terribly here and there. But most members of insect life here were absorbed in their own affairs and ignored the humans. There was an ant-city, whose foot-long warriors competed with the humans as scavengers. There were the bees, trying to eke out a livelihood from the great, cruciform flowers of the giant cabbage-plants and the milkweeds when water-lilies in the swamps did not bear their four-foot blooms. Wasps sought their own prey. Flies were consumers of corruption, but even the flies two feet in length would shy away from a man who waved his arms at it. So this valley had seemed to these people to be a truly admirable place.

But a fiend had entered it. As the gray light grew stronger the shivering folk looked terrifiedly about them. There were only twenty of the people now. Two weeks before there had been thirty. In a matter of days or less, there would be none. Because the valley had been invaded by a great gray furry spider!

*

There was a stirring, not far from where the man-folk trembled. Small, inquisitive antennae popped into view among a mass of large-sized pebbles. There was a violent stirring, and gravel disappeared. Small black things thrust upward into view and scurried anxiously about. They returned to the spot from which they had emerged. They were ants, opening the shaft of their city after scouting for danger outside. They scratched and pulled and tugged at the plug of stones. They opened the ant-city's artery of commerce. Strings of small black things came pouring out. They averaged a foot in length, and they marched off in groups upon their divers errands. Presently a group of huge-jawed soldier-ants appeared, picking their way stolidly out of the opening. They waited stupidly for the workers they were to guard. The workers came, each carrying a faintly greenish blob of living matter. The caravan moved off. The humans knew exactly what it was. The green blobs were aphids—plant lice: ant-cows—small creatures sheltered and guarded by the ants and daily carried to nearby vegetation to feed upon its sap and yield inestimable honeydew.

Something reared up two hundred yards away, where the thin mist that lay everywhere just barely began to fade all colorings before it dimmed all outlines. The object was slender. It had a curiously humanlike head. It held out horrible sawtoothed arms in a gesture as of benediction—which was purest mockery. Something smaller was drawing near to it. The colossal praying mantis held its pose, immovable. Presently it struck downward with lightning speed. There was a cry. The mantis rose erect again, its great arms holding something that stirred and struggled helplessly, and repented its unconsonanted outcry. The mantis ate it daintily as it struggled and screamed.

The humans did not watch this tragedy. The mantis would eat a man, of course. It had. The only creatures immune to its menace were ants, which for some reason it would not touch. But it was a mantis' custom after spotting its prey to wait immobile for the unlucky creature to come within its reach. It preferred to make its captures that way. Only if a thing fled did the mantis pursue with deadly ferocity. Even then it dined with monstrous deliberation as this one dined now. Still, mantises could be seen from a

119

distance and hidden from. They were not the terror which had driven the humans even from their hiding-places.

It had been two weeks since the giant hunting-spider had come through a mountain pass into this valley to prey upon the life within it. It was gigantic even of its kind. It was deadliness beyond compare. The first human to see it froze in terror. It was disaster itself. Its legs spanned yards. Its fangs were needle-sharp and feet in length—and poisoned. Its eyes glittered with insatiable, insane blood-lust. Its coming was ten times more deadly to the unarmed folk than a Bengal tiger loose in the valley would have been.

It killed a man the very first day it was in the valley, leaving his sucked-dry carcass, and going on to destroy a rhinoceros-beetle and a cricket—whose deep-bass cries were horrible—and proceeded down the valley, leaving only death behind it. It had killed other men and women since. It had caught four children. But even that was not the worst. It carried worse, more deadly, more inevitable disaster with it.

Because, bumping and bouncing behind its abdomen as it moved, fastened to its body with cables of coarse and discolored silk, the hunting-spider dragged a burden which was its own ferocity many times multiplied. It dragged an egg-bag. The bag was larger than its body, four feet in diameter. The female spider would carry this burden—cherishing it—until the eggs hatched. Then there would be four to five hundred small monsters at large in the valley. And from the instant of their hatching they would be just such demoniac creatures as their parents. They would be small, to be sure. Their legs would span no more than a foot. Their bodies would be the size of a man's fist. But they could leap two yards, instantly they reached the open air, and their inch-long fangs would be no less envenomed, and their ferocity would be in madness, in insanity and in stark maniacal horror equal the great gray fiend which had begot them.

The eggs had hatched. Today—now—this morning—they were abroad. The little group of humans no longer hid in the mushroom-forests because the small hunting-spiders sought frenziedly there for things to kill. Hundreds of small lunatic demons roamed the valley. They swarmed among the huge toadstools, killing and devouring all living things large and small. When they encountered each other they fought in slavering, panting fury, and the survivors of such duels dined upon their brothers. Small truffle-beetles died, clicking futilely. Infinitesimal grubs, newly hatched from butterfly eggs and barely six inches long, furnished them with tidbits. But they would kill anything and feast upon it.

A woman had died yesterday, and two small gray devils battled murderously above her corpse.

Just before darkness a huge yellow butterfly had flung itself agonizedly aloft, with these small dark horrors clinging to its body, feasting upon the juices of the body their poison had not yet done to death.

And now, at daybreak, the humans looked about despairingly for their own deaths to come to them. They had spent the night in the open lest they be trapped in the very forests that had been their protection. Now they remained in clear view of the large gray murderer should it pass that way. They did not dare to hide because of that ogreish creature's young, who panted in their blood-lust as they scurried here and there and everywhere.

As the day became established, the clouds were gray—gray only. The night-mist thinned. One of the younger women of the tribe—a girl called Saya—saw the huge thing far away. She cried out, choking. The others saw the monster as it leaped upon and murdered a vividly colored caterpillar on a milkweed near the limit of vision. The milkweed was the size of a tree. The caterpillar was four yards long. While the enormous victim writhed as it died, not one of the humans looked away. Presently all was still. The hunting-spider crouched over its victim in obscene absorption. Having been madness incarnate, it now was the very exemplar of a horrid gluttony.

Again the humans shivered. They were without shelter. They were without even the concept of arms. But it was morning, and they were alive, and therefore they were hungry. Their desperation was absolute, but desperation to some degree was part of their lives. Yet they shivered and suffered. There were edible mushrooms nearby, but with the deadly small replicas of the hunting-spider giant roaming everywhere, any movement was as likely to be deadly as standing still to be found and killed. The humans murmured to one another, fearfully.

But there was the young man called Burl, who had been lost from his tribe and had found it again. The experience had changed him. He had felt stirrings of atavistic impulses in recent weeks—the more especially when the young girl Saya looked at him. It was not normal, in humans conditioned to survive by flight, that Burl should feel previously unimagined hunger for fury—a longing to hate and do battle. Of course men sometimes fought for a particular woman's favor, but not when there were deadly insects about. The carnivorous insects were not only peril, but horror unfaceable. So Burl's sensations were very strange. On this planet a courtship did not usually involve displays of valor. A man who was a more skillful forager than the foot-long ants was an acceptable husband. Warriors did not exist.

Burl did not even know what a warrior was. Yet today the sullen, unreasonable impulses to conduct what he could not quite imagine were very strong. He knew all the despairing terror the others felt. But he also was hungry. The sheer doom that was upon his group did not change the fact that he wanted to eat, nor did it change the fact that he felt queer when the girl Saya looked at him. Because she was terrified, the same sort of atavistic process was at work in her. She looked to Burl. Men no longer served as protectors against enemies so irresistible as giant spiders. It was not possible. But when Burl realized her regard his chest swelled. He felt a half-formed impulse to beat upon it. His new-found reasoning processes told him that this particular fear was different in some fashion from the terrors men normally experienced. It was. This was a different sort of emergency. Most dangers were sudden and either immediately fatal or somehow avoidable. This was different. There was time to savor its meaning and its hopelessness. It seemed as if it should be possible to do something about it. But Burl was not able, as yet, to think what to do. The bare idea of doing anything was unusual, now. Because of it, though, Burl was able to disregard his terror when Saya regarded him yearningly.

*

The other men muttered to each other of the sudden death in the mushroom thickets. No less certain death now feasted on the dead yellow caterpillar. But Burl abruptly pushed his way clear of the small crowd and scowled for Saya to see. He moved toward the nearest fungus-thicket. An edible mushroom grew at its very edge. He marched toward it, swaggering. Men did not often swagger on this planet.

But then he ceased to swagger. His approach to the mingled mass of toadstools and lesser monstrosities grew slower. His feet dragged. He came to a halt. His impulse to combat conflicted with the facts of here and now.

His flesh crawled at the thought of the grisly small beasts which now might be within yards. These thickets had been men's safest hiding-places. Now they were places of surest disaster.

He stopped, with a coldness at the pit of his stomach. But as it was a new experience to be able to have danger come in a form which could be foreseen, so Burl now had a new experience in that he was ashamed to be afraid. Somehow, having tacitly undertaken to get food for his companions, he could not bring himself to draw back while they watched. But he did want desperately to get the food in a hurry and get away from there.

He saw a gruesome fragment of a tragedy of days before. It was the emptied, scraped, hollow leg-shell of a beetle. It was horrendously barbed. Great, knife-edged spines lined its edge. They were six inches in length. And men did not have weapons any more, but they sometimes used just such objects as this to dismember defenseless giant slugs they came upon.

Burl picked up the hollow shell of the leg-joint. He shook it free of clinging moulds—and small things an inch or two in length dropped from it and scurried frantically into hiding. He moved hesitantly toward the edible mushroom which would be food for Saya and the rest. He was four yards from the thicket. Three. Two. He needed to move only six feet, and then slice at the flabby mushroom-head, and he would be at least an admirable person in the eyes of Saya.

Then he cried out thinly. Something small, with insane eyes, leaped upon him from the edge of a giant toadstool.

It was, of course, one of the small beasts which had hatched from the hunting-spider's egg-bag. It had grown. Its legs now spanned sixteen inches. Its body was as large as Burl's two fists together. It was big enough to enclose his head in a cage of loathesomeness formed by its legs, while its fangs tore at his scalp. Or it could cover his chest with its abominableness while its poison filled his veins, and while it feasted upon him afterward....

He flung up his hands in a paralytic, horror-stricken attempt to ward it off. But they were clenched. His right hand did not let go of the leg-section with its razor-sharp barbs.

The spider struck the beetle-leg. He felt the impact. Then he heard gaspings and bubblings of fury. He heard an indescribable cry which was madness itself. The chitinous object he had picked up now shook and quivered of itself.

PLANET NIGHTMARE

The spider was impaled. Two of its legs were severed and twitched upon the ground before him. Its body was slashed nearly in half. It writhed and struggled and made beastly sounds. Thin, colored fluids dripped from it. A disgusting musky smell filled the air. It strove to reach and kill him as it died. Its eyes looked like flames.

Burl's arm shook convulsively. The small thing dropped to the ground. Its remaining legs moved frantically but without purpose.

It died, though its leg continued to twitch and stir and quiver.

Burl remained frozen, for seconds. It was an acquired instinct; a conditioned reflex which humans had to develop on this world. When danger was past, one stayed desperately still lest it return. But Burl's thoughts were now not of horror but a vast astonishment. He had killed a spider! He had killed a thing which would have killed him! He was still alive!

And then, being a savage, and an animal, as well as a human being, he acted according to that highly complicated nature. As a savage, he knew with strict practicality that it was improbable that there was another baby spider nearby. If there had been, they would have fought each other. As an animal, he was again hungry. As a human being, he was vain.

So he moved closer to the toadstool-thicket and put his hand out and broke off a great mass of the one edible mushroom at the edge. A noisesome broth poured out and little maggots dropped to the ground and writhed there in it. But most of what he had broken off was sound. He turned to take it to Saya. Then he saw the dropped weapon and the spider. He picked up the weapon.

The spider's legs still twitched, though futilely. He spiked the small body on the beetle-leg's spines. He strode back to the remnant of his tribe with a peculiar gait that even he had not often practiced.

It was rather more pronounced than a swagger. It was a strut.

They trembled when they saw the dead creature he had killed. He gave Saya the food. She took it, looking at him with bright and intense eyes. He took a part of the mushroom for himself and ate it, scowling. Thoughts were struggling to form in his mind. He was not accustomed to thinking, but he had done more of it than any other of the pitiful group about him.

He felt eyes watching him. There were five adult men in this group besides himself, and six women. The rest were children, from gangling

124

adolescents to one mere infant in arms. They were a remarkably colorful group at the moment, had he only known it. The men wore yellow-and-gold-brown loin-cloths of caterpillar-fur, stripped from the drained carcasses of creatures that the formerly resident clothed spider had killed. The women wore cloaks of butterfly-wing, similarly salvaged from the remnants of a meal left unfinished by a finicky or engorged praying mantis. The stuff was thick and leathery, but it was magnificently tinted in purples and yellows.

Time passed. The mushroom Burl had brought was finished. Some eyes always explored the clear ground around this group. But other eyes fixed themselves upon Burl. It was not a consciously questioning gaze. It was surely not a hopeful one. But men and women and children looked at him. They marveled at him. He had dared to go and get food! He had been attacked by one of the creatures who doomed them all, but he was not dead! Instead, he had killed the spider! It was marvelous! It was unparalleled that a man should kill anything that attacked him!

*

The doomed small group regarded Burl with wondering eyes. He brushed his hands together. He looked at Saya. He wished to be alone with her. He wished to know what she thought when she looked at him. Why she looked at him. What she felt when she looked at him.

He stood up and said dourly:

"Come!"

She moved timidly and gave him her hand. He moved away. There was but one way that any human being on this planet would think to move, from this particular spot just now—away from the still-feasting gigantic horror whose offspring he had killed. The folk shivered near the edge of the first upward slope of the valley wall. Burl moved in that direction. Toward the slope. Saya went with him.

Before they had gone ten yards a man spoke to his wife. They followed Burl, with their three children. Five yards more, and two of the remaining three adult men were hustling their families in his wake also. In seconds the last was in motion.

Burl moved on, unconscious of any who followed him, aware only of Saya. The procession, absurd as it was, continued in his wake simply because it had begun to do so. A skinny, half-grown boy regarded Burl's

125

stained weapon. He saw something half-buried in the soil and moved aside to tug at it. It was part of the armor of a former rhinoceros-beetle. He went on, rather awkwardly holding a weapon which might have been called a dagger, eighteen inches long, except that no dagger would have a hand-guard nearly its own length in diameter.

They passed a struggling milkweed plant, no more than twenty feet high and already scabrous with scale and rusts upon its lower parts. Ants marched up and down its stalk in a steady, single file, placing aphids from the ant-city on suitable spots to feed, and to multiply as only parthenogenic aphids can do. But already on the far side of the milkweed, an ant-lion climbed up to do murder among them. The ant-lion was the larval form the lace-wing fly, of course. Aphids were its predestined prey.

Burl continued to march, holding Saya's hand. The reek of formic acid came to his nostrils. But that was only ants. The slope grew steeper. Massacre began behind him on the tree-sized milkweed. The ant-lion which even when it was but half an inch long, on Earth, could bite through the skin of a man—the ant-lion reached the pasturing cows. It plunged into slaughter. It was demoniac. It was such ghastly ferocity that the eggs from which its kind hatched were equipped, each one, with a plastic column to hold it well away from the object on which the clutch of eggs were laid. But for this precaution by the maternal lace-wing fly, the first of her brood to hatch would devour its unhatched brothers and sisters. This ant-lion charged into the placidly feeding aphids on the milkweed plant. It seized one and crushed it, holding it aloft so that the juices of its body would pour into the ant-lion's mouth. Almost instantly, it seemed, the mild-eyed aphid was a shrunken empty sack. The ant-lion seized another. The remaining aphids fed placidly while their enemy did vast slaughter among them.

Clickings and a shrill stridulation sounded. Warrior-ants climbed with stupid ferocity to offer battle.

Burl moved on to a minor eminence. He reached its top and looked sharply about him with the caution that was the price of existence on this world. Two hundred feet away, a small scurrying horror raged and searched among the rough-edged layers of what on other worlds was called paper-mould or rock-tripe. Here it was thick as quilting, and infinitesimal creatures denned under it. The sixteen-inch spider devoured them, making gluttonous sounds. But it was busy, and all spiders are relatively short-sighted.

Burl turned to Saya—and realized that all the human folk had followed him. One of the adults was reaching fearfully for part of a discarded cricket-shell in the ground. He tore free an emptied, sickle-shaped jaw. It was curved and sharp and deadly if properly wielded. The man had seen Burl kill something. He tried vaguely to imagine killing something himself. He was not too successful. Another man tugged at the ground. The skinny boy was practicing thrusts with his giant dagger.

Two of the adults were armed, without any clear idea of what to do with their arms. But Burl knew, now.

He regarded them angrily. He had not meant to desert them, or even to take Saya permanently from among them. Humans had little enough of satisfaction on this planet. The scared company of their kind was one of the most important. So Burl did not resent that they had followed him. He did resent that they were near when he wanted to talk to Saya in what he did not yet think of as lover-like seclusion.

They halted, regarding him humbly. They had been hungry, and he had found food for them. They had been paralyzed by terror, and he had dared to move. So they moved with him. They might have followed anybody else, but only Burl had initiative—so far. They trustfully waited to follow and to imitate him for so long as panic numbed their ability to think for themselves.

Burl opened his mouth to shout furiously at them. But it was not a good idea for humans to draw attention. Spiders did not hunt by scent, but sound sometimes drew them. Burl closed his mouth again, in a taut straight line. The men looked at him supplicatingly. They had never been lost, and so had never learned to think even a little. Burl had learned to think in a rudimentary fashion and now he suddenly perceived that it was pleasing to have all the tribe regard him so worshipfully, even if not in quite the same fashion as Saya. He was suddenly aware that even as Saya had obeyed him when he told her to come with him, they would obey. He had, at the moment, no commands to give, but he immediately invented one for the pleasure of seeing it carried out.

"*I carry sharp things,*" he said sternly. "I killed a spider. Go find *sharp things* to carry."

127

PLANET NIGHTMARE

They were a meek and abject folk, and they were desperately in need of something to do to take their minds from the uselessness of doing anything at all.

They moved to obey. Saya would have loosened her hand and obeyed, too, but Burl held her beside him. One of the women, with a child three years old, laid the child down by Burl's feet while she went fearfully to seek some fragment of a dead creature, that would meet Burl's specification of sharpness.

Burl heard a stifled scream. A ten-year-old boy stood paralyzed, staring in an agony of horror at something which had stepped from behind a misshapen fungoid object.

It was a pallidly greenish creature with a small head and enormous eyes. It was a very few inches taller than a man. Its abdomen swelled gracefully into a pleasing, leaf-like shape. The boy faced it, paralyzed by horror, and it stood stock-still. Its great, hideously spiny arms were spread out in a pose of pious benediction.

It was a partly-grown praying mantis, not very long hatched. It stood rigid, waiting benignly for the boy to come closer. If he fled, it would fling itself after him with ferocity beside which the fury of a tiger would seem kittenish. If he approached, its fanged arms would flash down, pierce his body, and hold him inextricably fast by the spikes that were worse than trap-claws. And of course it would not wait for him to die before it began its meal.

The small party of humans stood frozen. They were filled with horror for the boy. They were cast into a deep abyss of despair by the sight of a half-grown mantis, because if there was one such miniature insect-dinosaur in the valley, there would be many others. Hundreds of others. This meant there had been a hatching of them. And they were as deadly as spiders.

*

But Burl did not think in such terms just now. Vanity filled him. He had commanded, and he had been obeyed. But now obedience was forgotten because there was this young praying mantis. If men had ever thought of fighting such a creature, it could have destroyed any number of them by pure ferocity and superiority of armament. But Burl raged. He ran toward the spot. Even mantises were sometimes frightened by the unexpected. Burl seized a lumpish object barely protruding from the ground. It looked like a rock. It was actually a flattened ball-fungus, feeding on the soil through thin white threads beneath it. Burl wrenched it free and hurled it furiously at the young monster.

Insects simply do not think. Something came swiftly at it, and the mantis flashed its ghastly arms to seize and kill its attacker. The ball-fungus was heavy. It literally knocked the mantis backward. The boy fled frantically. The insect fought crazily against the thing it thought had assailed it.

The humans gathered around Burl hundreds of yards away—again uphill. The slope of the mountain-flank was marked here. They gathered about Burl because of an example set by the woman who had left her three-year-old child behind. Saya, in the unfailing instinct of a girl for a small child, had snatched it up when Burl left her. Then she had joined him because the instinct which had made her obey him in starting off—it was not quite the same instinct which moved the others—also bade her follow him wherever he went. The mother of the child went to retrieve her deposit. Other figures moved cautiously toward him. The tribe was reconvened.

The floor of the valley seemed a trifle obscured. The mist that hung always in the air made it seem less distinct; less actual; not quite as real as it had been.

Burl gulped and said sternly:

"Where are the sharp things?"

The men looked at one another, numbly. Then one spoke despairingly, ignoring Burl's question. "Now," said the man dully, "there was not only the hunting-spider in the valley, but its young. And not only the young of the hunting-spider, but the young of a mantis ... It was hard to stay alive at the best of times. Now it had become impossible ..."

Burl glared at him. It was neither courage nor resolution. He had come to realize what a splendid sensation it was to be admired by one's fellows. The more he was admired, the better. He was enraged that people thought to despair.

"I," said Burl haughtily, "am *not* going to stay here. I go to a place where there are neither spiders nor mantises. Come!"

He held out his hand to Saya. She gave the child to its mother and look his hand. Burl stalked haughtily away, and she went with him. He went uphill. Naturally. He knew there were spiders and mantises in the valley. So many that to stay there was to die. So he went away from where they were.

Burl had found out that adulation was enjoyable and authority delectable. He had found that it was pleasant to be a dictator. And then he had been disregarded. So he marched furiously away from his folk, in exactly the fashion of a spoiled child refusing to play any longer. He happened to march up the mountainside toward the cloud-bank that he considered the sky. He had no conscious intent to climb the mountain. He did not intend to lead the others. He meant to sulk, by punishing them through the removal of his own admirable person from their society. But they followed him.

So he led his people upward. It has happened on other planets, in other manners. Most human achievements come about through the daring of those who strive.

*

The sun was very near. It shone upon the top of the cloud-bank and the clouds glowed with a marvelous whiteness. It shone upon the mountain-peaks where they penetrated the clouds, and the peaks were warmed, and there was no snow anywhere despite the height. There were winds here where the sun shone. The sky was very blue. At the edge of the plateau where the cloud-bank lay below, the mountainsides seemed to descend into a sea of milk. Great undulations in the mist had the seeming of waves, which moved with great deliberation toward the shores. They seemed sometimes to break against the mountain-wall where it was cliff-like, and sometimes they seemed to flow up gentler inclinations like water flowing up a beach.

All this was in the slowest of slow motion, because the cloud-waves were sometimes miles from crest to crest.

The look of things was different on the plateau, too. This part of the unnamed world, no less than the lowlands, had been seeded with life on two separate occasions. Once with bacteria and moulds and lichens to break up the rocks and make soil of them, and once with seeds and insects-eggs and such living things as might sustain themselves immediately upon hatching. But here on the heights the conditions were drastically unlike the lowland tropic moisture. Different things had thrived, and in quite different fashion.

Here moulds and yeasts and rusts were stunted by the sunlight. Grasses and weeds and trees survived, instead. This was an ideal environment for plants that needed sunlight to form chlorophyll, and chlorophyll to make use of the soil that had been formed. So here was vegetation that was nearly Earth-like. And there was a remarkable side-effect on the fauna which had been introduced at the same time and in the same manner as down below. In coolness which amounted to a temperate climate there could be no such frenzy of life as formed the nightmare-jungles in the lowlands. Plants grew at a slower tempo than fungi, and less luxuriantly. There was no adequate food-supply for large-sized plant-eaters. Insects which were to survive in sunshine could not grow to be monsters. Moreover, the nights were chill. Many insects grow torpid in the cool of a temperate-zone night, but warm up to activity soon after sunrise. But a large creature, made torpid by cold, will not revive so quickly. If large enough, it will not become fully active until close to dusk. On the plateau, the lowland monsters would starve in any case. But more—they would have only a fraction of a day of full activity.

There was a necessary limit then, to the size of the insects that lived above the clouds. The life on the plateau would not have seemed horrifying at all to humans living on other planets. Save for the absence of birds to sing and lack of a variety of small mammals, the untouched sunlit plateau with its warm days and briskly chill nights would have impressed most men as an ideal habitation.

But Burl and his companions were hardly prepared to see it that way at first glimpse. Certainly if told about it beforehand, they would have viewed it with despair.

But they did not know beforehand. They toiled upward, their leader moved by such ridiculous motives as have sometimes caused men to achieve greatness throughout all history. Back on Earth, two great continents were discovered by a man trying to get spices to conceal the gamey flavor of half-spoiled meat. The power that drives mile-long space-craft, and that lights and runs the cities of the galaxy, was first developed because it could be used in bombs to kill other men. There were precedents for Burl leading his fellows into sunshine merely because he was angered that they ceased to admire him.

The trudging, climbing folk were high above the valley, now. The thin mist that was never absent anywhere had hidden their former home, little by little. They climbed a steeply slanting mountain-flank. The stone was mostly covered by ragged, bluish-green rock-tripe in partly overlapping sheets. Such stuff is always close behind the bacteria which first attack a rock-face. On a slope, it clings while soil is washed downward as fast as it forms. The people never ate it. It produced frightening cramps. In time they would learn that if thoroughly dried it can he soaked to pliability again and cooked to a reasonable palatability. But so far they knew neither dryness nor fire.

Nor had they ever known such surroundings as presently enveloped them. A slanting, stony mountainside which stretched up frighteningly to the very sky. Grayness overhead. Grayness, also, to one side—the side away from the mountain. And equal grayness below. The valley in which they lived could no longer be seen at all. Trudging and scrambling up the interminable incline, the people of Burl's personal following gradually realized the strangeness of their surroundings. As one result, they grew sick and dizzy. To them it seemed that the solid earth had tilted, and might presently tilt further. There was no horizon, but they had never seen a horizon. So they felt that what had been *down* was now partly *behind*, and they feared lest a turning universe let them fall ultimately toward the grayness they considered sky.

In this frightening strangeness, their only consolation was the company of their fellows. To stop would be to be abandoned in this place where all values were turned topsy-turvy. To go back—but none of them could imagine descending again to be devoured as one-third of their number already had been. If Burl had stopped, his followers would have squatted down and shivered together miserably, and waited for death. They had no thought of adventure nor any hope of safety. The only goodnesses they could imagine were food and the nearness of other humans. They clung together, obsessed by the dread of being left alone.

Burl's motivation was no longer noble. He had started uphill in a fit of sulks, and he was ashamed to stop.

They came to a place where the mountain-flank sank inward. There was a flat area, and behind it there was a winding cañon of sorts, like a vast crack in the mountain's substance. Burl breasted the curving edge, and walked on level ground. Then he stopped short.

The mouth of the cañon was perhaps fifty yards from the lip of the downward slope. There was this level space, and on it there were toadstools and milkweed, and there was food. It was a small, isolated asylum for life such as they were used to. It could have been that here they could have found safety. But it wasn't that way.

*

They saw the web at once. It was slung from between the opposite cliff-walls by cables two hundred feet long. Its radiating cables reached down to anchorages on stone. The snare-threads, winding out and out in that logarithmic spiral which men on other planets had noted thousands of years before—the snare-threads were a yard apart. The web was set for giant game. It was empty now, but Burl searched keenly and saw the tight-rope-cable leading from the very center of the web to a rocky shelf some fifty feet above the cañon's floor. At its end he saw the spider. It waited there, almost invisible against the stone, with one furry leg touching the cable that led to its waiting-place so that the slightest touch on any part of the web would warn it instantly.

Burl's followers accumulated behind him. They stared. They knew, of course, that a web-spider will not leave its snare under any normal circumstances. They were not afraid of that. But they looked at the ground between the web and themselves.

It was a charnel-house of murdered creatures. Half-inch-thick wing-cases of dead beetles. The cleaned-out carcasses of other giants. The ovipositor of an ichneumon-fly—six feet of slender, springy, deadly-pointed tube—and abdomen-plates of bees and draggled antennae of moths and butterflies.

Something very terrible lived in this small place. The mountainsides were barren of food for big flying things. Anything which did fly so high for any reason would never land on sloping, foodless stone. It would land here. And very obviously it would die. Because something—something—killed them as they came. It denned back in the cañon where they could not see. It dined here.

The humans looked and shivered. All but Burl. He deliberately chose for himself a magnificent lance grown by one dead creature for its own defense. He pulled it out of the ground and cleaned it with his hands. He seemed absorbed, but he was terribly aware of the inner depths of the cañon. He was actually pretending, for the sake of what he believed his dignity.

Fearfully, the other humans imitated him in choosing weapons from the armory of the devoured. Then Burl stalked grandly to one side and began to climb again. His people followed him in numbed silence. They were filled with dread, but it was not quite terror. Insects do not stalk their prey. The deadly unseen monster of the cañon had not attacked them. Therefore, it did not know they were there. And therefore they were safe from it until it appeared. But none of them desired to stay.

The slope lessened here, and half a mile further on there was a small thicket of mushrooms. From within it came the cheerful loud clicking of some small beetle, arrived at this spot nobody could possibly know how, but happily ensconced in a twenty-yard patch of jungle above a hollow that had gathered soil through the centuries. There were edible mushrooms in the thicket.

The humans ate. Naturally. And here they realized that they were no longer doomed by the creatures in the valley. Since their climb began they had seen no dangerous thing except the one gigantic, motionless web-spider. They had left the valley and its particular dangers behind.

A man exclaimed in naïve astonishment. He was eating raw mushroom at the moment, and his mouth was full. But abruptly it occurred to him that their doom was lifted. He mentioned the fact in a sort of startled wonder.

"We will stay here," he added happily. "There is food."

And Burl regarded him with knitted brows. Burl was well on the way to becoming spoiled. He had tasted power over his folk, and he found himself jealous of any decision by anybody else.

"I go on," he said haughtily. "Now! You may stay behind if you wish—alone!"

He broke off food for the journey. He held out his hand to Saya. He went on. And again he went upward because to go back was to go to the cañon of the unknown killer. And his folk docilely followed him. They did not really reason about it. To follow him had become a pattern, more or less precarious. In time it could become a habit. Over a period of years it could even become a tradition.

The procession marched on and up. Burl noticed that the air seemed clearer, here. It was not the misty, quasi-transparent stuff of the valley. He could see for miles to right and left, and the curvatures of the mountain-face. But he could not see the valley.

Then he realized that the cloud-bank he saw was finite—an object. He had never thought of it specifically before. To him it had seemed simply the sky.

Now he saw an indefinite lower surface which yet definitely hid the heights toward which he moved. He and his followers were less than a thousand feet below it. It appeared to Burl that presently he would run into an obstacle that would simply keep him from going any further. But until that happened he obstinately continued to climb.

The thing which was the sky appeared to stir. It moved. A little higher, and he could see that there were parts of it which were lower than he was. They moved also. But they did not approach him. And he had no experience of anything inimical which did not plunge upon its victims. Therefore he was not afraid.

In fact, a little later he observed that the whiteness retreated before him, and he was pleased. Weak things such as humans fled aside when predators approached. Here was something which fled aside at his approach. His followers undoubtedly observed the same phenomenon. He had killed a spider. He was a remarkable person. This unknown white stuff was afraid of him.

Burl, with bland conceit, marched confidently through the cloud-bank, ever climbing. At its thickest, he could see only feet in each direction, but always when he advanced threateningly upon opacity, it cleared before him.

Presently the gray light grew brighter. Burl and his folk were accustomed to a shadowless illumination such as fungi could endure—the equivalent of a heavily overcast day on an Earth-type planet. Now the mist about him took on a luminosity which was of a different kind. Suddenly he noticed the silence. He had never known even comparative silence before in all his life. His ears had been assailed every minute since he had been born by a din which was the noise of creatures. By stridulations, by chirpings, by screams, or at the least by the clicking of armor or the deep-toned pulsations of wings. He had always lived in the uproar of frenzied struggle. Now, that hellish chorus of shrieks and cries and mating-calls was cut off. The lower surface of the cloud-bank reflected it. Burl and his people moved upward through an unparalleled stillness.

PLANET NIGHTMARE

They fell silent, marveling. They heard each other's movements. They could hear each other's voices. But they moved in a vast quietness over stones which here were not even lichen-covered, but glistened with wet. And all about them a golden glow hung in the very air. Stillness, and quietude, and golden light which grew stronger and stronger and stronger....

It was very remarkable when they came up through the sea of mist upon a shore of sunshine, and saw blue sky and sunlight for the first time. The light smote upon their pink skins and brilliantly colored furry garments. It glinted in changing, ever-more-colorful flashes upon the cloaks made of butterfly wings. It sparkled upon the great lance carried by Burl in the lead, and the quite preposterous weapons borne by his followers.

The little party of twenty humans waded ashore through the last of the thinning white stuff which was cloud. They gazed about them with blinking, wondering, astounded eyes. The sky was blue. There was green grass. And there was sound. The sound was of wind blowing in the trees and sunshine.

They heard insects, too, but they did not know what it was they heard. The shrill, small musical whirrings, the high-pitched small cries which made up a strange new elfin melody, were totally strange. All things were novel to their eyes, and an enormous exultation filled them. From deep-buried ancestral memories, they knew that this was somehow right, was somehow normal. And they breathed clean air for the first time in many generations.

Burl even shouted, in triumph, and his voice rang echoing among rocks. The plateau rang with the shouting of a man in triumph!

*

They had enough food for days. They had brought it from the isolated thicket not too far beneath the clouds. Had they found other food immediately, they would have settled down comfortably, in the fashion normal to creatures whose idea of bliss is a secure hiding-place and food on hand. Somehow they believed that this high place was secure. But it was not a hiding-place. And though they did accept, with the simplicity of children and savages, that they had no enemies here, their first quest, nevertheless, was for a place in which they could conceal themselves.

They found a cave. It was small to hold all of them, so that they would be crowded in it, but, as it turned out, that was fortunate.

At some time it had been occupied by some other creature, but the dirt which floored it had settled flat and there were no recent tracks. It retained faint traces of an odor which was unfamiliar but not unpleasant. It had no connotation of danger.

Ants stank of formic acid plus the musky odor of their particular city and kind. One could tell not only the kind of ant but what hill they came from, from a mere sniff at a well-traveled ant-trail. Spiders had their own hair-raising odor. The smell of a praying-mantis was acrid, and of beetles decay, and of course those bugs whose main defense was smell gave off an effluvium which tended to strangle all but themselves.

The cave's smell was quite different. The humans thought vaguely that it might be another kind of man. Actually, it *was* the smell of a warm-blooded animal. But Burl and his fellows knew of no warm-blooded creatures but themselves.

They had come above the clouds a bare two hours before sunset—of which they knew nothing. For an hour they marveled, staying close together. They were astounded by the sun, more particularly since they could not look at it. But presently, being savages, they accepted it with the matter-of-factness of children.

They could not cease to wonder at the vegetation about them. They were accustomed only to gigantic fungi, and a few feverishly growing plants striving to flower and bear seed before being devoured. Here they saw many plants, and at first no insects at all. However, they looked only for the large things they were accustomed to.

They were astounded by the slenderness of the plants. Grass fascinated them, and weeds. A large part of their courage came from the absence of debris upon the ground. In the valley, the habitation of a trapdoor spider was marked by grisly trophies—armor emptied of all meat but not yet rotted by the highly specialized bacteria which flourished upon chitin. The hunting-ground of even a mantis was marked by discarded, transparent beetle-wings and sharp spiny bits of armor, and mandibles not tasty enough to be consumed. Here, in the first hour of their exploration, they saw no sign that any insect from the lowlands had ever come to this place at all. But they interpreted the fact quite correctly as rarity, rather than complete absence of huge creatures blundering up into the sunlight.

PLANET NIGHTMARE

They were relieved that they had found a cave. There was no thicket of trees close-growing enough to shelter them. They were ludicrously amazed when they found that trees were hard and solid, because the fungi they knew were easily cut by sawtoothed tools. They found nothing to eat, but they were not yet hungry. They did not worry about it while they still had bits of edible mushroom from their climb.

When the sun sank low and the crimson colorings filled the western horizon, they shivered. They watched the glory of their first sunset with scared, incredulous eyes. Yellows and reds and purples reared toward the zenith. It became possible to look and gaze directly at the sun. They saw it descend behind something they could not guess at. Then there was dark.

The fact stunned them. So night came like this!

Then they saw the stars as they winked singly into being. And the folk from the lowland crowded frantically into the cave with its faint odor of having once been occupied. They filled the cave tightly. But Burl was somewhat reluctant to admit his fear, and Saya lingered close to him. They were the last to enter.

*

Nothing happened. Nothing. The sounds of evening continued. They were strange but infinitely soothing and somehow what night-sounds ought to be. Burl and the others could not possibly analyze it, but for the first time in many generations they were in an environment really similar to that intended for their race. It had a rightness and a goodness about it which was perceptible for all its novelty. And because Burl had once been lost from his tribe, he was capable of estimating novelties a little better than the rest.

He listened to the night-noises from close by the cave's small entrance. He heard the breathing of his tribesmen. He felt the heat of their bodies, keeping the crowded enclosure warm enough for all. Saya was close beside him. She held fast to his arm for reassurance. He was wakeful, and thinking very busily and very painfully.

Saya was filled with a tumult that was combined fear of the unknown and relief from much greater fear of the familiar ... and warm, proud memories of the sight of Burl leading and commanding the others, and memories of the look and feel of sunshine, and pictures of sky and grass and trees which she had never seen before. Emotion-filled memories of Burl as he killed a spider! Flinging a ball-fungus at a hatchling mantis, saving a young boy. Grandly leading the others up the mountainside which it had never occurred to anybody else to climb. Keeping onward sternly when it seemed that the solid ground had twisted and would drop them into a misplaced sky. And now, between her and the doorway to the strange and very beautiful night outside.

Saya felt an absorbed, impassioned, delectable disquiet from the touch of Burl's arm beneath her fingers.

He stirred. She whispered a question.

"I am going out," he murmured in her ear. "I wish to see the lights. To see if they come nearer, or move."

It had occurred to him that the first few stars they had seen glowed in darkness like the giant fireflies of the valley. They were comparable in size to all the enlarged insect kingdom. They were a yard and more in length, and sometimes at night they soared and wheeled above the lowland fungus jungles, and the segmented larval females of their kind, which never grew wings, grew frantic at the sight. They climbed recklessly upon the flat tops of toadstools and waved their dimmer twinned lanterns at the flying males.

But this was not the lowland. Burl freed his arm from Saya's fingers. He crept through the constricted opening of the cave, carrying his lance before him. He already had a vague idea that it should be not only an instrument but a weapon. He imagined stabbing enemy creatures with it—but only vaguely, as yet.

He stood upright in the open air. There was coolness. Night had fallen, but only a little while since. There were smells in the air such as Burl had never smelled before—green things growing, and the peculiar clean odor of wind that has been bathed in sunshine, and the peculiarly satisfying fragrance of coniferous trees.

But Burl raised his eyes to the heavens. He saw the stars in all their glory, and he was the first man in at least forty generations to look at them from this planet. There were myriads upon myriads of them, varying in brightness from stabbing lights to infinitesimal twinklings. They were of every possible color. They hung in the sky above him, immobile and unthreatening. They had not come nearer. They were very beautiful.

Burl stared. And then he noticed that he was breathing deeply, with a new zest. He was filling his lungs with clean, cool, fragrant air such as men were intended to breathe from the beginning, and of which Burl and many others had been deprived. It was almost intoxicating to feel so splendidly alive and unafraid.

There was a rustling. Saya stood beside him, trembling a little. To leave the others had required great courage. But she had come to realize that if any danger befell Burl she wished to share it. So she had come. They shared the starlight.

They heard the nightwind and the orchestra of night-singers. They wandered aside from the cave-mouth, and Saya found completely primitive and wholly atavistic pride in the courage of Burl, who was actually not afraid of the dark! Her own uneasiness became merely something to give more savor to her pride in him. She stayed close beside him, not only for reassurance but also for joy in being close to him.

Presently they heard a new sound in the night. It was very far away and not in the least like any sound they had ever heard before. It changed in pitch. Insect-cries do not. It was a baying, yelping sound. It rose in pitch, and held the higher note, and abruptly dropped in pitch before it ceased. Minutes later it came again.

Saya shivered, but Burl said thoughtfully:

"That is a good sound."

He didn't know why. Saya shivered once more. She said reluctantly:

"I am cold."

It had been a rare sensation in the lowlands. It came only after one of the infrequent thunderstorms, when wetted human bodies were exposed to the gusty winds that otherwise rarely blew there. But here the nights grew cold, after sundown. The heat in the ground radiated to outer space at night, not being trapped by a layer of clouds. Before dawn, the temperature would be close to freezing, though anything worse than a light fleeting hoar-frost would be rare on this plateau.

The two of them went back to the cave. It was warm there. The cave was so packed with humans that their body-heat kept the air from growing chill. Burl and Saya crouched among the rest, and became drowsy and comfortable. Presently Saya dropped off to sleep, her hand trustfully in Burl's.

But he remained awake for a long time, blinking. He thought of the stars, but they were too strange. He thought of the trees and grass. But most of the impressions of this upper world were so remote from previous knowledge that he could only accept them as they were and defer reflection upon them until later. But he did feel an enormous complacency, what with having brought his followers to an effective paradise of safety, and having arrived at a completely satisfactory emotional status with Saya.

But the last thing he actually thought about, before his eyes blinked shut in sleep, was that yelping noise he had heard in the night. It was totally novel in kind, yet there was something buried among his racial heritages that told him it was good.

*

Burl was first awake of all the tribesmen and he looked out into a cold and pallid grayness. He saw trees. One side of the cluster was brightly lighted, the other side was dark. He heard tiny singing noises of the creatures of this place. Presently he crawled out of the cave to scout for danger.

The air was biting in its chill. It was an excellent reason why giant insects could not survive here, but it was particularly invigorating as he breathed it in. Then he summoned courage to move to where he could peer at the source of this strange light.

He saw the top of the sun as it peered above the eastern cloud-bank. The sky grew lighter. He blinked at the sun and saw it rise more fully into view. He thought to look upward, and the stars that had bewildered him were nearly gone.

He ran to call Saya.

The rest of the tribe waked as he roused her. One by one they followed, to watch their first sunrise. The men and women gaped at the sun as it filled the east with colorings and rose above the seemingly steaming layer of clouds and then appeared to spring free of the horizon and swim on upward.

The children blinked and shivered and crept to their mothers for warmth. The women enclosed them in their cloaks, and they thawed and peered out once more at the glory of sunshine and the day. Soon, though, they realized that warmth came from the glaring body in the sky. The children presently discovered a game. It was the first game they had ever played, and it consisted simply of running into a shaded place until they shivered, and then of running out into the sunshine again where they were warm. Until this dawning they had never been free enough from fear to play at all. But this discovery of the nightly chill and of the utility of cloaks for warmth up here as well as it had been against the nightly rain of the lowlands, was a specific suggestion of the value of clothing. Which was to have another significance, a short time later.

In this first dawn of their experience, the tribesmen ate of the edible mushroom they had brought up the mountain-flank. But there was not an indefinite amount of food left. Burl shared the meal Saya brought him. She touched him fondly. But he regarded his happy fellows with something like a scowl. They were quite contented, and they had for the moment no need of his guidance. They did not look to him for orders. And Burl wanted attention.

He spoke abruptly.

"We do not want to go back to the place we came from," he said sternly. "We must look for food here, so we can stay for always. Today we look for food."

It was a seizure of the initiative. It was the linking of what the folk most craved with obedience to Burl. It was the instinct of a leader. The eating men murmured agreement. There was a certain definite idea of goodness—not moral virtue, but of the desirable—becoming associated with what Burl did and what Burl commanded. His tribe was becoming a group of which he was the leader, rather than only a loose association held together only by the fear of solitude.

He led them exploring as soon as they had eaten. All of them, of course. None had yet become confident enough to be left behind. They straggled irregularly behind Burl and Saya. They came to a brook and regarded it with amazement. There were no leeches. No fungus. No swiftly drifting islands of scum. It was clear. Greatly daring, Burl tasted it and it was water, but such as he had never tasted before. It was clean, fresh, sparkling water, not fouled by drainage through mould or rust.

The rest of the tribe tasted. A child slipped on a muddy place and sat down hard on white stuff that yielded and almost splashed. The child howled. Saya picked it up. Then she looked where it had been for spines or small stinging things.

She stared blankly.

She went to Burl with a tiny white thing in her hand. It was a mushroom. But it was a *tiny*, clean, appetizing object. Saya had no words for it. She was amazed.

Burl smelled it carefully. He tasted it. And it was actually no more and no less than a normal mushroom, growing in a shaded place upon enormously rich soil. It had been protected from sunlight, but it had not the means nor the stimulus to become a monster.

Burl ate it. He carefully composed his features. Then he announced the find to his followers.

There was food here, he told them. But in this splendid world to which he had led them, food was small. There would be no great enemies here, but the food would have to be sought in small objects rather than great ones. They must look at this place and seek others like it, where food would be found....

The tribesmen were doubtful. But they plucked mushrooms—whole ones!—instead of merely breaking off parts of their tops. In deep astonishment they recognized miniatures of what they had known only in gigantic forms. They tasted. The tiny mushrooms had the same savor, but they were not coarse or stringy or tough like the giants. They melted in the mouth! Life in this place to which Burl had led them was delectable! Truly the doings of Burl were astonishing!

When a child found a beetle on a leaf, and they recognized it, they were entranced, for instead of being bigger than a man and a thing to flee from, it was less than an inch in size and helpless against them. From that moment on, they would follow Burl anywhere and obey him in any matter, in the happy conviction that he could do nothing that was not desirable in all respects.

The belief, of course, was not quite accurate. Tender tiny mushrooms as a staple, instead of the tough and chewy provender they were used to, in time would cause them to have toothaches. But they could not anticipate it, and it was actually very far away in time.

They struggled after Burl through vast patches of bushes with thorns on them. They were not used to thorns, and they deeply distrusted the bushes and even the glistening fruit on them, which eventually they would know were blackberries. Near midday they heard noises in the distance.

The sounds were made up of cries of varying pitch, some of which were sharp and abrupt, and others longer and less loud. The people did not understand them in the least. They could have been the cries of human beings, but they were assuredly not cries of pain. Also they were not language. They seemed to convey an impression of enormous, zestful excitement. They had no overtone of horror. And Burl and his folk had known of no excitement among insects except the frenzy of ferocity. They were unable to imagine even the nature of the tumult.

To Burl the cries seemed to have somewhat the timbre of the yelping sounds he had heard the night before. And he had felt instinctively drawn to that sound. He liked it.

He led the way boldly in the direction of the noise. And presently he came out of breast-high weeds with Saya close behind him and the others trailing. He emerged upon a space of bare stone, a little upraised. He looked down into a small and grassy amphitheater. The tumult came from its center.

A pack of dogs were joyously attacking something that Burl could not see clearly. They *were dogs*. They barked zestfully, and they yelped and snarled and yapped in a dozen different voices, and they darted at the unseen something and darted away, and they were having a thoroughly enjoyable time, though it might not be so good for the thing they attacked.

One of them saw the humans and stopped stock-still and barked. The others whirled and saw the humans as they came out into view. The tumult ceased entirely.

There was silence. The men for the first time saw creatures with only four legs. They had never before seen any moving thing with fewer than six—except men. Spiders had eight. The dogs did not have mandibles. They did not act like insects.

And the dogs saw men, whom they had never seen before. Much more important, they smelled men. And the difference between man-smell and that of insects was vast. Through many generations the dogs had not smelled anything with warm blood save their own kind. The difference in smell between insect and man was so great that the dogs did not react with suspicion, but with curiosity. This was an unparalleled smell. It was even a good smell.

The dogs regarded the men with their heads on one side, sniffing them in the deepest possible amazement—amazement so intense that they could not feel hostility. One of them whined a little because he did not understand.

*

Peculiarly enough, it was a matter of topography. The plateau which reached above the clouds rose with a steep slope from the valley in which Burl and the others had lived. To westward, however, the highland was subject to an indentation which almost severed it. No more than twenty miles from where Burl's group had climbed to sunshine, there was a much more gradual slope downward. There, mushroom-forests grew almost to the cloud-layer. From there, giant insects strayed up and onto the plateau itself. They could not live on the plateau, of course. There was no food for their insatiable hunger. Especially at night, there was no warmth to keep them active. But they did stray from their normal environment, and some of them reached the sunshine, and perhaps some of them blundered back down to their mushroom-forests again. But those that did not find their way back were chilled to torpor during their first night on the highland. They were only partly active on the second day if, indeed, they were active at all. And few or none recovered from the second night of cold. Certainly none kept their full ferocity and deadliness. And this was how the dogs survived.

Unquestionably the dogs were descended from dogs on the wrecked ship—name now unknown—which had landed on this planet some forty-odd human generations since. The humans had no memories of that ship, and the dogs had surely no traditions. But perhaps because those early dogs had less of intellect, they had possessed more useful instincts. Perhaps dogs were bred by the first desperate generations of humans, to warn them against dangers. But no human civilization could survive the environment of the lowlands. The humans inevitably reverted to the primitive. The environment was not one in which dogs could survive, so somehow they took to the heights. Perhaps dogs survived their masters. Perhaps some were abandoned or driven away. But dogs had reached the heights. And they did survive because of the simple fact that giant insects blundered up after them—and could not survive the proper environment for dogs and men.

There was even a reason why they had not multiplied excessively. The food-supply was limited. When there were too many dogs, their attacks on

145

stumbling insects were more desperate, and made earlier before ferocity of the insects was lessened. And more dogs died. So there was a specific adjustment of the dog population to the food-supply. There was also a selection of those intelligent enough not to attack foolishly, but not of those whose cowardice left them out of conflict altogether.

These dogs who regarded men with their heads cocked on one side were excellent dogs. Intelligent dogs. They did not attack anything imprudently, and they knew it was not necessary to be more than wary of insects in general. Even spiders, unless they were very newly arrived from the lowlands. So the attitude of men and dogs was that of astonished curiosity rather than that of instant fear or rage. Burl knew that the shaggy, bright-eyed creatures were unlike insects. Actually, they behaved strikingly like men. They were estimating these strange beings, men. Insects never estimated. Those that were not carnivorous had no interest in anything but food, and those that were carnivorous lumbered insanely into battle the instant any prey came to their notice. The dogs did neither. They sniffed. They considered. They were amazed.

Burl said harshly to his group:

"Stay here!"

He walked slowly down into the amphitheater. Saya, disregarding his order, followed him instantly. The dogs moved warily aside. But they raised their noses and sniffed—long, luxurious sniffs. The smell of humankind was a good smell. Dogs had gone hundreds of generations without having it in their nostrils. But before that there were thousands of generations of dogs to whom that smell was a fulfillment.

Burl reached the object the dogs had been attacking. It lay on the grass, throbbing painfully. It had come up from the world below. It was the larva of an azure-blue moth which spread ten-foot wings at nightfall. The time for its metamorphosis was near, and it had gone blindly in search of a place where it could spin its cocoon safely and change to its winged form. It had come to another world—the world above the clouds. It could find no proper place. Its stores of fat had protected it a little from the chill. But the dogs had found it.

Burl considered. It was the custom of wasps to sting creatures like this within a certain special spot—marked for them apparently by a tuft of dark fur.

Burl thrust his lance into that particular spot. The creature died quickly and without agony. The thought to kill was an inspiration, which was the result of continued adventuring. Burl cut off meat for his tribesmen. The dogs offered no objection. They were well-fed enough. Burl and Saya, together, carried the meat back to the blinking tribesfolk. On the way they passed within two yards of a dog which regarded them with extreme intent and almost a wistful expression. Their smell did not mean game. It meant—something the dog struggled dumbly to remember.

"I have killed the thing," said Burl, in the tone of one speaking to an equal. "You can go and eat it now. I took only part of it."

The dog wagged its tail—and then backed away as if in confusion. After all, matters had not yet progressed to cordiality.

The humans consumed what Burl had brought them. Most of the dogs went to the feast Burl had left. Presently they were back. They had no reason to be hostile. They were fed. The humans offered them no injury. The humans smelled good. The dogs were fascinated by their smell.

Presently they were close about the humans. They were not insects. They were interested. The humans were extremely interested in anything which was interested in them. It was a wholly novel experience. It was the feeling Burl had felt in becoming the tribal leader. Now every human felt a little of it, in the intent regard of the dogs. And everything else was so strange that it was possible to accept anything without question. Even the possible friendliness of unparalleled creatures which assuredly were not of a kind with past enemies.

A similar state of "mind" existed among the dogs.

Saya had more meat than she desired. She looked about among the humans. All were well supplied. She tossed it to a dog. He jerked away alertly, and then sniffed at the meat where it had dropped. A dog can always eat. He ate it.

"I wish you would talk to us," said Saya hopefully.

The dog wagged his tail.

"You do not look like us," said Saya interestedly, "but you act as we do. Not as the—monsters!"

The dog looked at meat in Burl's hand. Burl tossed it. The dog caught it with a quick snap, swallowed it, wagged his tail briefly and came closer. It was a completely incredible action, but dogs and men were blood-kin on this planet. Besides, there was subconscious racial-memory instinct in friendship between man and dog. It was not overlaid by any past experience of either. They were the only warm-blooded creatures on this world. It was kinship felt by both.

Burl stood up and spoke politely to the dog. He addressed him with the same respect he would have given to another man. In all his life he had never felt equal to an insect, but he felt no arrogance toward this dog.

He felt superior only to other men.

"We are going back to our cave," he said politely. "Maybe we will meet again."

He led his tribe back to the cave in which they had spent the previous night. The dogs followed, ranging on either side. They were well-fed, with no memory of hostility to any creature which smelled like men. They had instinct and intelligence. The latter part of the return to the cave—if anybody had been qualified to notice—was remarkably like a group of dogs taking a walk with a group of people. It was companionable. It felt remarkably right.

That night Burl left the cave, as before, to look at the stars. This time Saya went with him, gladly. But as they emerged from the cave-entrance there was a stirring. A dog rose and stretched itself elaborately, yawning the while. When Burl and Saya walked aside from the cave, the dog trotted amiably with them.

They talked to it, embarrassed. And the dog seemed pleased. It wagged its tail.

When morning came the dogs were still waiting hopefully for the humans to come out. They appeared to expect the humans to take another nice long walk, on which they would accompany them. It was a brand-new satisfaction they did not wish to miss. After all, from a dog's standpoint, humans were made to take long walks with, among other things. The dogs greeted the humans with tail-waggings and cordiality.

*

The friendship of the dogs assured the humans' new status in life. They had ceased to be fugitive game for any insect murderer. They had hoped to be unpursued foragers. But, joined to the dogs, they were raised to the estate of hunters. The men did not domesticate the dogs. They made friends with them. The dogs did not subjugate themselves to the men.

They joined them, at first tentatively and then with worshipful enthusiasm. And the partnership was so inherently right that within a month it was as if it had been always. And indeed, except for a few centuries, for them, it had.

The humans had made a permanent encampment by then. There were a few caves at an appropriate distance from the slope up which most wanderers from the lowlands came. The humans moved into the caves. A child found the chrysalis of a giant butterfly, whose caterpillar form had so offensive an odor that the dogs had not attacked it. But when it emerged from the chrysalis, humans and dogs together assailed it before it could take flight. They ended with warm approval of each other. The humans had great wings with which to make cloaks. And men wore cloaks now—shorter than the women's—but cloaks. They were very useful against the evening chill. When one dawning a vast outcry of dogs awoke the humans, Burl led the rush to the spot, and his great lance did execution which the dogs appeared to admire. Burl wore a moth's feathery antennae, now, bound to his forehead like a knight's plumes. They were very splendid.

In a single month their entire way of life went through a revolution. The ground was often thorny. A man pierced his foot, and bandaged it with a strip of wing-fabric so he could walk. The injured foot was more comfortable to walk with than the well one. Within a week women were busily contriving divers forms of footgear, to achieve the greatest comfort. One day Saya admired glistening red berries and tried to pluck them, and they stained her fingers. She licked the fingers—and berries were added to the tribe's menu. A veritable orgy of experimentation began. And this was a state of affairs which is very, very rare among human beings. A tribe with an established culture and tradition cannot change without disaster. But men who have abandoned their old ways and are seeking new ones can go far.

Already the dogs were established as sentries and watchmen and friends to every one of the humans. By now mothers did not feel alarmed if a child wandered out of sight. There would be dogs along. No danger could approach a child without vociferous warning from the dogs. Men went hunting, now, with zestful tail-wagging dogs as companions in the chase. By the time a stray monster from the lowlands reached this area, it was dazed and half-numbed by at least one night of bitter cold. Even spiders could not find energy to leap. They fought like fiends, but sluggishly. Men could kill them while dogs kept their attention. Burl killed one the third week on the plateau. He was nerved to the deed by a peculiar feeling that he must be worthy of the courage of the dogs with him at the time.

And presently, while their way of life was still fluid, the permanent pattern of civilization on the nightmare planet was settled. Burl and Saya went out early one morning with the dogs, to hunt for meat for the village. Hunting was easiest in the morning while creatures strayed up the night before were still numbed. Often, hunting was merely butchery of an enfeebled monster to whom any sort of movement was enormous effort.

This morning the humans moved briskly. The dogs roamed exuberantly through the brush before them. They were five miles from the village when the dogs bayed game some distance ahead. And Burl and Saya ran to the spot hand in hand—which was something of a change from their former actions at the thought of a giant creature of the insect kind—and found the dogs dancing and barking around one of the most ferocious and most ghastly of the carnivorous beetles. It was not too large, to be sure. Its body might have been four feet long, but its horrid mandibles added three feet more.

Those scythe-like objects gaped wide—opening sidewise as a beetle's jaws do—and snapped hideously, swinging about as the dogs dashed at them. The legs were spurred and spiked and armed with dagger-like spines. Burl plunged into the fight.

The great gaping mandibles clicked and clashed. They were capable of disemboweling a man or snapping a dog's body in half without effort. There were whistling noises as the beetle breathed through its abdominal spiracles. It fought furiously, making frantic plunges at the dogs who dashed in and out to torment and bewilder it while they created the most zestfully excited of uproars.

There was something beside this conflict that Burl and Saya should have noticed, but they were instantly intent. The other thing was quite unparalleled. There had been nothing else like it on this planet in many hundreds of years. It moved slowly above the plateau as if examining it. It was half a dozen miles away and perhaps a mile higher when Burl and Saya prepared to intervene professionally on behalf of the dogs. Then it swerved and moved directly toward them. It moved swiftly.

But it was silent, and they did not know at all. Burl leaped in with a lance-thrust at the tough integument where an armored leg joined the body. He missed, and the monster whirled. Then Saya flashed her cloak before the beetle, so that it seemed a larger and nearer antagonist. As the creature whirled again, Burl thrust once more and a hind-leg crumpled.

Instantly the thing limped crazily. A beetle does not use its legs like four-legged creatures. It moves the two end legs on one side with the center leg on the other, so that always it is braced on an adjustable tripod. But it cannot adjust readily to crippling.

A dog snatched at a spiny lower leg and crunched and darted away. The expressionless, machine-like horror uttered a formless, deep-bass cry and was spurred to all possible ferocity. The fight became a thing of furious movement and uproar, with Burl striking once at a multiple eye so the pain would deflect it from a charge on Saya, and Saya again deflecting it with her cloak and once breathlessly trying to strike it with her shorter spear.

Then the beetle sank to the ground, all three legs on one side crippled. The remaining three thrust and thrust and struggled terribly and suddenly it was on its back, still striking its gigantic jaws frantically in the hope of murder. But Burl stabbed home between two armor-plates where a ganglion was almost exposed. A thrust killed it instantly.

Burl and Saya smiled at each other. There was a monstrous sound of splintering trees. They whirled. The dogs pricked up their ears. One of them barked defiantly.

*

Something huge—truly huge!—settled to the ground a bare hundred yards away. It was metal, and there were ports, and it was utterly beyond experience, because, of course, there had been no spaceship landings on this planet in forty-odd human generations. But as Burl and Saya stared blankly at it, a port opened, and men came out, and they waved hopefully to the two barbarically attired figures who had been seen fighting a monster with the help of dogs. Which meant some sort of civilization.

The dogs confirmed it. They sniffed. These, also, were men. And Burl and his tribe had this smell, and were friends. So the dogs trotted forward with the self-confident cordiality of dogs on excellent terms with men—and there was no question of friendship. None at all. The men came forward joyously to talk to Burl and Saya.

There were difficulties, of course. But Burl and Saya had the calm composure of savages, and the alertness of people who are changing the pattern of their lives of their own volition—and finding it very pleasant—and things went swimmingly. There was, on the spaceship, an "educator." They invited Burl to put it on his head. He obliged. And very shortly he understood a new language, and was equipped with a very considerable fund of general information. Among the items of information was the fact that presently he would have a splitting headache—he did—and that the making of records for an educator was so different that it required generations to get all the facts and knowledge for a single type of education down in permanent form.

All of which fitted admirably into the arrangements that the men on the spaceship were anxious to make, and Burl was enthusiastically willing to accede to. He and his folk knew the creatures of the lowlands as nobody else could possibly know them. No electronic educator could possibly make a record making available that knowledge in less than two generations—maybe three. Therefore—

*

The nightmare world swims in space about its nearby sun. It has a name now, but it does not matter. It has a city on it, which probably matters less. It is a curious city, though. The people in it wear gorgeous colored fur, and cloaks of butterfly wings. The least of the people in that city wear garments which would fetch fortunes on other inhabited worlds. In fact, such garments do. But it is most practical for Burl, and Saya, and their followers to wear such garments. There is no day but that a small, winged flying craft rises from the city to go silently over the plateau until it reaches the space above the cloud-bank, and then dives down into it. It is wise for the occupants and the operators of such small craft to wear garments like the other humans on this planet. They are recognized, that way, when garments such as most planets find suitable would make them seem strange.

They want to be recognized, in the jungles and the noisesome valleys of the lowlands. There are other humans down there. The people of the city, of course, bring their fellows out as fast as they can find them. There is a session with an educator—and a splitting headache afterward—and very soon the folk who have hidden from monsters all their lives are zestfully hunting them with dogs. Presently they are hunting them with flying machines.

It is a nice arrangement. The search for more people in the lowlands is a prosperous business even when it is unsuccessful. The wings of white morph butterflies bring the highest price, but even a common swallow-tail is riches enough. And the fur of caterpillars—duly processed—goes into the holds of the regular spaceliners with the same care given elsewhere to jewels and platinum.

But the nightmare planet has not become a merely sordid place of business. What comforts and what luxuries spaceships can bring are available enough, to be sure. But the city on the plateau, and the homes of the barbarically clad inhabitants are not places to which invitations are coveted for the luxury of them. The planet is a sportman's paradise.

Not long since, the Planet President of *Surmor III* was a guest in Burl's dwelling. Burl is all hard muscle, despite his graying hair, and he and Saya have fitted very beautifully into the sort of civilization that turned out to be congenial to them. They have grown children now, and their home is quite fit to entertain a World President in its richness. But it is small—the size they want it to be.

The atmosphere is oddly informal. There are self-respecting and amiable dogs nearly everywhere. The World President of *Surmor III* was inclined to be stand-offish at first. But he is a sportsman, like Burl. And since the last hunting trip, he is very respectful. After all, there are few planet leaders who will, as they do, for pure sporting joy of the hunt, fight the mastodon-sized tarantula of the lowlands with nothing but a spear—and win.

But Burl does.